CARLO COLLODI'S

THE ADVENTURES OF

PINOCCHIO

translated and adapted by Marianna Mayer

illustrations by Gerald McDermott

FOUR WINDS PRESS

NEW YORK

ACKNOWLEDGMENTS

I wish to express my gratitude to Gerald Gottlieb, Curator of Early Children's Books, the Pierpont Morgan Library, New York, and Sharyl Smith for their valuable guidance during my background research for the illustrations. My thanks also to Dr. Karen Nelson Hoyle, Curator, The Kerlan Collection, University of Minnesota, for allowing me access to the many historic editions of THE ADVENTURES OF PINOCCHIO in the Collection.

G. McD.

I would like to express my deep appreciation to my assistant, Lisa Malchiodi Smith, for her invaluable help during the translation of the original text. I am very grateful to the Pierpont Morgan Library in New York City, and in particular to Sharyl Smith and Gerald Gottlieb, for the courtesy shown me while I researched the rich material they hold on PINOCCHIO. Special thanks to Gerald McDermott whose encouragement throughout the entire project helped immeasurably. And last but not least, my gratitude to my editor and publisher, Judith Whipple, for the patience and support I have come to continually rely upon.

M.M.

Library of Congress Cataloging in Publication Data. Mayer, Marianna. The adventures of Pinocchio. Based on: Le avventure di Pinocchio. Summary: The adventures of a talking wooden marionette whose nose grew whenever he told a lie. [1. Fairy tales. 2. Puppets and puppet-plays—Fiction] I. Collodi, Carlo, 1826-1890. Avventure di Pinocchio. II. McDermott, Gerald. III. Title. PZ8.M4514Ad [Fic] 81-66856 AACR2 ISBN 0-590-07546-2 to Lucia Coletti Brawley

PREFACE

The Adventures of Pinocchio is both touching and humorous, but it is not until one reads the original Italian text that one really appreciates the wit and sensitivity of its author, Carlo Collodi. The Italian text makes it clear that Pinocchio is every child full of dreams and schemes, and one's sympathy is with Pinocchio during his many misadventures. He is the brash, willful, know-it-all kid whose schemes only get the better of him time and time again. It is his exuberant spirit that puts him in conflict with good and evil. This small wooden boy symbolizes the child that parents and teachers watch with dismay, wondering if he will grow into a devil or a saint. But the path Pinocchio takes is marked *transformation.* He finally achieves human form after learning to combine his boldness and bravery with compassion and concern for others. His adventures, his soul's journey, follow a course to this end. He is like the very best in all of us, young and old, developing his true potential by going through his mistakes to reach wisdom. The reward for Pinocchio is the realization of his heart's desire which is to become a full human being.

Almost every generation of children has had its own version of *Pinocchio.* Through reading various English versions and translations, I found a few were strictly scholarly, line-for-line translations, while others gave barely a nod to the basic story line and dedicated themselves instead to shortening and reworking the story. Unfortunately, some of the loveliest versions have long since gone out of print. Most of what remains available to children today, in print or on television or in film animation, has come to bear so little resemblance to the original story that it is now time to go back to the source. This volume presents modern children with a straightforward but not oversimplified version, containing the complete adventures of Pinocchio retold directly from the original Italian.

The style of this text attempts to preserve the Italian flavor without recourse to archaisms. The idiom is today's, but wherever possible the Italian idiomatic meaning has been sustained. The old Italian proverb, "traduttore traditore," was in my mind as I worked. Pirandello, the Italian playwright, often cited this same proverb. He felt all translators were traitors and believed they unwittingly betrayed the original sense of his work. Here is a very simple example from an early scene in *Pinocchio*, where I attempted to preserve the visual sense of Collodi's meaning. Geppetto arrives at Master Cherry's home with an "idea" about carving a puppet that will dance and make death-defying leaps. The word *idea* has been used in English versions to describe Geppetto's extraordinary thought, the very thought that launches the story and Pinocchio's adventures. Though in part the word is correct, it is not as evocative as the Italian idiom used. To literally translate the idiom in English the meaning would be something like this: The thought was raining in Geppetto's head. . . . There is in our own language a good comparison—a "brainstorm." This then was the word I used and, though it is not a word-for-word translation, it was expressive enough to satisfy what the Italian idiom means to convey.

Therefore, my approach was dual; on the one hand I worked from direct translation of the original text, on the other I improvised when an Italian idiomatic phrase could be replaced with an English colloquialism. The result is both objective and subjective, a translation and an adaptation, as I interpreted freely where it best suited the material. The goal was to enliven this classic tale and allow contemporary children to make the wonderful characters, and especially Pinocchio, their own.

M.M.

CHAPTER I

Once there was a piece of wood. A casual glance would prove it to be quite ordinary in almost every way. A solid log of wood, in fact, that one might place on the fire to warm oneself or use to make a piece of furniture.

This particular piece of wood remained for some time in the shop of a carpenter by the name of Master Cherry, who lived in a small village in Italy. The carpenter's real name was Antonio, but he was called Master Cherry by everyone for the tip of his nose was as bright and as round and as red as a ripe cherry.

This evening he had been working very hard on a table he was making. Searching in his woodpile, Master Cherry discovered this very piece of wood. He exclaimed, "Ah! This is just right. It will soon make a fine leg for my table."

Immediately he sat down and set to work on the wood with his chisel. "Look out!" a tiny voice cried suddenly. Bewildered, Master Cherry stopped and looked all around the room.

"Is there someone here?" he asked.

But he saw no one. He got up and looked in the closet. No one. Then he went to his cupboard. No one. He opened his shop door and looked down the dark, windy street, but there was no one there, either. He closed the door, shivering from the cold draft.

"I must have imagined I heard a voice," he decided.

So he set to work again, giving the piece of wood a sharp blow. "Oh! You hurt me," cried the same small voice.

Master Cherry's mouth dropped open and his tongue hung out nearly to his chin. His eyes looked as though they might pop from his head. "C-could it be that this piece of wood can cry like a baby?" he stuttered. "How *can* it be?" With both hands he took hold of the wood firmly. "If there is something in this wood, so much the worse for it. I'll teach it to frighten me!" he said, banging it against the wall. He paused to listen for any sound. Nothing.

Then he began to laugh. "Ha! How silly of me. There is absolutely nothing to be frightened of. Just as I thought all along."

He fluffed the wig he wore to cover his bald head and again began to chip away at the rough bark and smooth it with sandpaper.

"Stop! You're tickling me," that same little voice said, laughing.

Master Cherry was so shocked he fell off his chair. His face turned white, while his red nose changed to the color of a dark-purple grape.

"It's the devil's work!" he cried, trembling.

CHAPTER II

Just then there was a knock at the door.

"Come in," called Master Cherry, too shaken to rise from the floor.

Master Geppetto, an old friend, entered. When the children in the village wished to tease him, they often called him Polendina. In Italy, *polendina* is a cornmeal mush. Geppetto's matted yellow wig was exactly the same color. To be called "Mush Head" never failed to drive Geppetto into a furious rage.

"Good evening, Antonio," said Geppetto. "What are you doing sitting on the floor?"

"I am teaching the ants to read. What else?" he replied.

"Indeed, I hope it does them good," Geppetto answered with a smile.

"What brings you here this evening?" asked Master Cherry, easing himself up from the floor wearily.

"My two feet, of course," Geppetto said, laughing at his own joke.

When Master Cherry did not laugh with him, Geppetto went on quickly, saying happily, "Besides that, I have had a brainstorm! I am going to make a magnificent puppet that can dance, do tricks, and make death-defying leaps that will astonish everyone. Together we will travel the world. Who knows? Someday we may be famous!"

"Polendina the famous, indeed!" said that same mysterious voice.

Geppetto blushed red as a red-hot pepper when he heard himself called Polendina. In a voice like the growl of a wild animal he asked, "Why do you insult me, Antonio?"

Master Cherry nervously backed up. "Come now, my good friend, do you think I said it?"

"Who was it if not you? Are you saying *I* said it?" Geppetto shouted.

The air was scalded with Geppetto's anger. Since both old men had quick tempers, in no time angry words changed to angry blows. They began to pinch and bite and scratch at each other. At the end of the battle Master Cherry had Geppetto's yellow wig and Geppetto had Master Cherry's gray wig between his teeth.

"Give me back my wig," cried Master Cherry.

"Then give me mine and let's make peace," Geppetto suggested meekly.

The two old men exchanged wigs, shook hands, and vowed to be friends again.

"Now then, dear Geppetto, can I be any help to you?"

"Yes, that's why I came. I need a small piece of wood to carve this special puppet. Can you give me one?" asked Geppetto.

"I have one I would gladly give you," Master Cherry replied, only too happy to be rid of the troublesome wood.

At that moment, like a piece of slippery soap, the wood flew from Master Cherry's outstretched hand and struck a swift, harsh blow to Geppetto's knee.

"Oooh, you've crippled me! Is this the way you present a friend with a gift?" cried Geppetto.

"I didn't do it," Master Cherry said in desperation.

"Oooh, I suppose I did it to myself then!" Geppetto snapped, rubbing his painful knee.

"It is this wood's fault," Master Cherry tried to explain.

"Yes, I know it was the wood that hit me, but it was *you* who threw it!"

"I did not throw it!" Master Cherry replied angrily.

"Liar!"

"Geppetto, don't insult me or I will call you Mush Head," threatened Master Cherry.

"Ugly ape!" shouted Geppetto.

"Mush Head! Mush Head! MUSH HEAD!"

Once again tempers were too hot for words alone. As soon as Geppetto heard the hated name for a third time, he lost all sense of reason and he threw himself at Master Cherry. They brought up their fists and began to box, but, at their advanced age, neither was too steady. It was impossible to move in the small cluttered workroom without tripping over wood chips or unfinished tables and chairs. They stumbled and soon were rolling on the floor like two angry monkeys.

Finally, exhausted, they stopped. Since each had two more scratches and had lost two more buttons from their vest, it seemed to them both that the score was settled. They shook hands and Geppetto left for home with the mysterious piece of wood that would soon be a lively puppet.

CHAPTER III

The very next morning Geppetto began work on his puppet. As he worked, he wondered what he should name it.

"I once knew a whole family named Pinocchi. Pinocchio, the father. Pinocchia, the mother. Pinocchi, the children. They all did very well for themselves. The richest among them became a wealthy beggar. For good luck I will name my puppet after all of them. Pinocchio!" Geppetto announced proudly.

Then he also remembered that the word *pinocchio* means little mischiefmaker.

"Hmm, if I name him Pinocchio, he may turn out to be a little rascal," he worried.

But in the end he concluded that Pinocchio was a good-luck name.

It wasn't long before Geppetto had carved the wood into

the head of a boy. As he finished the eyes, Geppetto imagined they stared at him ominously. He tried to ignore them and continued to work on the nose. But the nose seemed to begin to grow. He chipped away at it, trying to shorten it, but still the nose remained longer than he wished. And the wooden eyes did not stop their curious staring.

"Wicked eyes of wood, why do you stare at me?" Geppetto asked at last, annoyed.

But Pinocchio did not answer. Then Geppetto finished the mouth. No sooner had he finished than the mouth stuck out its tongue at him.

"What's this? Have you no respect for your father?" The puppet did not answer. Again Geppetto pretended not to notice. Suddenly, he felt his wig slip from his head.

"What?" Geppetto jumped and looked around the room, only to find his old yellow wig on Pinocchio's wooden head. "Pinocchio, give me my wig immediately," Geppetto demanded, snatching his wig from the puppet. "Wicked son! You are not even finished and already you are making fun of your father."

Then Geppetto began work on the rest of the puppet—his body, his arms, his stomach, his legs, and his feet. When he was finished carving he gently guided Pinocchio around the room. At first the little wooden boy's legs were uncertain, but soon he

was able to walk on his own. Around and around the room he walked, then he hopped, then he skipped and then. . . .

"Stop! Stop! Someone catch him," Geppetto shouted, his pride suddenly turning to panic as he saw Pinocchio jump out the door and run into the street.

Geppetto tried to catch up while calling for help, but Pinocchio was much too fast for him. A Policeman heard the clatter of Pinocchio's wooden feet on the pavement and thought someone's horse had gotten loose. He planted himself firmly in the middle of the narrow street, determined to stop the creature from getting away.

When Pinocchio and the Policeman came face to face, the puppet tried to duck between the Policeman's legs, but he was quickly caught by the end of his very long nose. The Policeman turned him over to Geppetto, who was so angry that he took Pinocchio by the neck and began to shake him.

"Wait till I get you home. I will give you your very first spanking," Geppetto promised severely. When Pinocchio heard this, he fell on the ground and began to cry and plead for mercy.

"Poor boy," an onlooker observed. "I know Geppetto is a good man, but he is hard on boys."

"Yes, and he has a terrible temper," said another.

"I'll bet he ran away because Geppetto beats him," said another.

"Just a minute then," the Policeman said, reconsidering. "You had better come along with me for questioning, Geppetto."

Geppetto was taken into custody and Pinocchio was set free, to skip merrily back home.

CHAPTER IV

Ha, ha, ha, I'm free!" said Pinocchio, laughing as he walked into the house and slammed the door.

"Oh, you little fool," said a squeaky voice from the corner of the room.

"Whoever said that had better look out. I'm the master of this house now!" Pinocchio announced boldly.

On the wall stood a very large black Cricket, who wasn't the least bit impressed by Pinocchio's words. "Wicked boys who disobey their parents soon regret it, if they are not lucky enough to change," said the Cricket.

"Watch out, Cricket, before *you* regret it. This is my house. I want you to leave. Be quick about it, or you'll pay the consequences," Pinocchio said, not at all politely.

"I have lived in this house for more than one hundred years and I intend to remain. What do you plan to do, may I ask, now that you are free?" the Cricket said, completely ignoring Pinocchio's threats.

"Tomorrow I will leave here for good. If I'm here when my father returns he will make me go to school, and that means I will have to work hard, study, and take tests. But that's not the life for me. I want to play all the time. Every day will be a holiday and I will do what I please," boasted the puppet.

"You poor fool," the Cricket said patiently. "With that attitude you will never be happy until you learn that what you want must be earned to be enjoyed."

The puppet made an ugly face and said, "You are a bad-luck Cricket. The best life is the life without work. I will play morning, afternoon, and night. I'll eat when I please and I'll sleep when I choose. I'll dance if I like and take what I want—and I won't wait to be asked, either."

"For your information, all those who lead the life you describe end up at best either imprisoned or dead," the Cricket predicted solemnly.

"Watch out, Cricket, or you'll go too far. You'd better go while you have the chance," the puppet said angrily.

"Oh, I'm not afraid of a wooden head like you," the Cricket replied.

"Ah, this will teach you who winds up dead!" said Pinocchio. With that he threw a wooden mallet at the Cricket.

There wasn't another sound. Pinocchio shivered as he looked about the room, but he did not see the Cricket anywhere. "Cricket, where did you go?" Pinocchio asked, but there was no answer.

CHAPTER V

As night approached Pinocchio felt the first pangs of hunger. He began to search the room for food—in the drawer, in the cupboards—but he found nothing. The more he hunted, the hungrier he became. "Oh, just some bread, even a bit of stale crust, or even what a dog might leave on a bone, or some fish bones, or the stone from a cherry, just a small something to chew," he moaned. He felt empty, so he opened his mouth very wide and began to cry: "What a terrible disease hunger is. I know it is fatal. The Cricket was right. If I hadn't disobeyed my father I wouldn't have to die of hunger."

Just then he saw something white and smooth and round. He grabbed it, and as he turned it over in his hands, he kissed it. "An egg! How shall I eat it? I'll cook it, but how? Maybe I'll make an omelette, or maybe I should bake it? No, maybe it would be tastier if I fried it in a pan. I know, I'll eat it raw! No, no, I'll cook it. I'm too hungry to waste any more time thinking about it."

Pinocchio took a pan and placed it on the fire. Then he cracked the egg on the edge of the pan. "Thank you, Pinocchio, for setting me free," said a little Chick. She curtsied, fluffed her feathers, fluttered her wings, and flew out the window. Astonished, Pinocchio stood there holding the empty eggshell. There was nothing left to do but cry.

CHAPTER VI

At last Pinocchio dried his tears and decided to go to sleep. He sat down by the fire to keep warm and propped his feet up on the fireplace irons. As he slept, the heat from the fire was so hot that it charred his feet to ashes, but Pinocchio felt nothing. Instead, he slept soundly until the next morning, when there was a knock at the door.

"Let me in," Geppetto called.

When Pinocchio tried to get up, he fell to the floor.

"Father, I can't," Pinocchio called out. "The fire has eaten my feet." The puppet hopped and fell and made a terrible racket, but he could not get up.

Geppetto, already annoyed, gave up trying to get in through the door. Instead, he hoisted himself up the side of the house and crawled in through the window.

Geppetto's heart softened when he saw his little Pinocchio.

"Father, I will have to walk on my knees the rest of my life.

I've fed my feet to the fire, but *I'm* still hungry."

Geppetto reached into his pocket and produced three ripe pears. "These were to be my breakfast, but you may have them, my child," said Geppetto.

"Peel them for me," Pinocchio demanded.

"Peel them? How fussy you are. Eat them as they are." Pinocchio made an awful face, and Geppetto, reconsidering, peeled each one and placed all the scraps neatly in a pile on the table.

"Why do you save them, Father?" Pinocchio asked.

"Everything has some use," replied Geppetto.

Pinocchio ate the pears one by one. But just as he was about to throw each core away, Geppetto took it from him and placed it with the parings.

"Is there nothing more?" the puppet asked.

Geppetto shook his head.

"But I'm still hungry, Father."

"I have nothing else except these scraps," Geppetto said, pointing to the leftover parings.

"Nothing? Well, maybe I'll try some." Pinocchio took a bite, grimaced, but then proceeded to eat all that remained. Then he tapped his stomach. "I feel better," he announced.

"You see, my child, everything has some use in this world," Geppetto said.

CHAPTER VII

No sooner had Pinocchio's hunger been satisfied than he began to complain. "I still have no feet," he wailed.

"But if I make you another pair of feet, how do I know you will not run away again?" asked Geppetto.

"Never! I promise I won't, and I always keep my word," Pinocchio said innocently.

"That's what all children say when they want something."

"But I'm different from other children. I'm better!" Pinocchio insisted.

"We'll see. I'll make a bargain with you: I'll make you new feet if you will promise to go to school."

"Yes, Father. You'll see. I'll go to school and work hard," Pinocchio said sincerely.

"All right, then, I will begin at once." Geppetto took a small piece of wood and in no time carved a beautiful pair of new wooden feet. Then he told Pinocchio to close his eyes and sleep. Pinocchio did as he was told, but he only pretended to sleep. Geppetto took some glue and joined the new feet to Pinocchio's legs. They fit perfectly. As soon as Geppetto was finished Pinocchio jumped up and began to dance wildly around the room.

"Now, my son, you are ready to go to school."

"Wait, Father. I must have school clothes, or I can't go."

But Geppetto was much too poor to buy clothes for Pinocchio. So he made a suit from wrapping paper, a pair of shoes from the bark of a tree, and he molded a cap from some bread.

"Do I look like a gentleman?" asked Pinocchio.

"Yes, indeed you do, but remember it is not the fine clothes that make the gentleman, but the man himself. Now off to school."

"Wait. I can't go."

"What is the problem now?"

"I must have a school book."

"This *is* a problem," said Geppetto, shaking his head sadly because he had no money to buy one.

"Oh, well, then I can't go to school after all," said Pinocchio, relieved.

"Just a minute. I have an idea," Geppetto said, getting up from his chair. Without a word, he took his coat and went out the door.

In a little while he returned holding a new school book. Although it was snowing out, he did not have his coat.

"Where is your coat, Father?" the puppet asked.

"I sold it."

"Why?"

"There are more important things than coats, and, anyway, it made me too warm."

Pinocchio realized his father had sold his coat to buy him a school book. He threw his arms around Geppetto and said, "I will go to school and make you proud of me."

CHAPTER VIII

While Pinocchio walked to school, he made many plans. "I'll be a good student—the best. I'll study hard and. . . ." But just then he heard the sounds of drums and flutes playing in the distance. He started to follow the music and soon saw a crowd gathering around a brightly painted caravan.

"What's all the excitement?" Pinocchio asked a boy who rushed past him.

"It's the puppet theater," the boy answered.

Pinocchio followed after the boy, thinking, "I've never seen a puppet theater! Surely tomorrow is soon enough to go to school."

"Does it cost anything to see the show?" Pinocchio asked the boy.

"Nothing's free in this world—tickets cost five cents," the boy answered.

Pinocchio shook his head. "Can you lend me the money?"

"I don't lend money," said the boy.

"Well, maybe I could sell you something then."

"Like what?" the boy asked doubtfully.

"Ahh . . . how about my jacket?" the puppet said.

"What possible good would a paper jacket do me?" the boy replied, laughing.

"Then how about my shoes?"

"Wooden shoes! They would only be good for making a fire."

"How much would you give me for my cap?" Pinocchio asked, not willing to give up.

"Nothing! A cap made of bread! You would have better luck trying to sell it to a mouse than me."

Pinocchio was quiet for a few moments. His next idea presented him with a difficult decision. Finally, he suggested nervously, "Here, I'll sell you my new school book."

"No, I have my own," the boy replied.

A peddler who overheard the conversation interrupted. "I'll buy your book for five cents."

"Sold!" Pinocchio said, without a thought to anything but the puppet show. He bought a ticket and rushed into the theater and got a seat just as the play was about to begin.

There on stage were Arlecchino, a famous puppet from Venice, and Pulcinella from Naples. When they looked into the audience and saw Pinocchio they stopped their dialogue abruptly.

"Pinocchio!" Arlecchino shouted, pointing toward him.

"Yes, it *is* Pinocchio!" Pulcinella exclaimed.

"It is! It is! Our very own brother Pinocchio!" shrieked Signora Rosaura, as she peeked from a corner of the stage.

Then all the puppets came running out onto the stage to greet him as a brother.

"Pinocchio, come up. Come up and join us!" they all called together.

Pinocchio climbed up onto the stage, and all the puppets crowded around to welcome him. But the audience began to complain that, if the show was not going to continue, they should be given their money back.

The Puppet Master hurried out to the stage to see what all the confusion was about. He was a huge, powerful man with a long black beard that reached to the floor. His mouth was as wide and as large as an oven, and his eyes were mean black coals lit with fiery red-flamed centers. He held a long whip made of live snakes and he cracked it angrily. Indeed, he was altogether a terrifying sight, and everyone, including Pinocchio, fell silent instantly. The puppets shook with fear when the Master ordered them to begin the show. Then he turned his smoldering gaze to Pinocchio. "How dare you disrupt my theater!" he growled in a monstrous voice.

Pinocchio could hardly find the courage to answer. "Believe me, Master, I meant no harm," he pleaded.

"Enough! We'll settle this tonight after the performance." He carried Pinocchio off the stage and hung him from a hook on the wall.

When the play was over the Puppet Master began to prepare a fire to cook his meal. He shouted to two of his puppets, "Bring that puppet Pinocchio to me. My fire is not hot enough. I will use his dried wooden body to feed my flames."

The two puppets wanted to protest, but their fear of the Puppet Master prevented them. Instead, they went to carry out his command and they soon returned dragging Pinocchio, who was crying bitterly. "Please, someone, save me! I don't want to burn!"

CHAPTER IX

Although the Puppet Master, whose name was Fire-Eater, looked fierce, actually he had a kind heart. He heard Pinocchio's cries and was moved to pity. Though he tried to ignore his feelings, he could not. Suddenly he let out an enormous sneeze. One of the puppets who was holding Pinocchio whispered, "Don't worry, my friend, that sneeze means Fire-Eater feels sorry for you."

Fire-Eater narrowed his black eyes and looked at the pitiful sight of Pinocchio.

"Stop your crying. Your tears give me a terrible case of the sneezes. I feel a spasm that I . . . ah . . . ah . . . AH-CHOOO!"

"May God bless you, Master," said Pinocchio.

"Thank you. Have you any parents?" Fire-Eater asked, as he pinched his nose to hold back another sneeze.

"Only my dear father, kind sir."

"How miserable your father would be if I used you for my fire. Oh well, instead I will have to use one of the other puppets to finish cooking my meat."

He called his guards to bring Arlecchino in Pinocchio's place. When Arlecchino was brought forward, he screamed in terror and fell to the floor. Pinocchio jumped in front of Fire-Eater and took hold of his long beard.

"Mercy!" cried Pinocchio. "I beg you to spare Arlecchino."

"Impossible. One of you must feed my fire if I am to finish cooking my roast."

Then Pinocchio made a gallant and courageous gesture.

"Come, guards! Tie my hands and feet so my body will not fight you, and throw me to the fire," he said bravely.

At these valiant words all the puppets began to cry. Fire-Eater sat as though made of ice. At first he appeared unmoved, but little by little he began to sniffle and then he let out a terrible bout of sneezes.

"Stop, stop! You are a brave puppet," he said, embracing Pinocchio.

Then, in a tiny frightened voice Arlecchino asked, "Am I to be spared, too?"

"Yes," Fire-Eater replied, sighing deeply. "I'll eat my roast half-cooked tonight." When the puppets heard this, they began to dance and sing. The festivities that followed lasted through the night and well into the morning.

CHAPTER X

The next morning, Fire-Eater called Pinocchio to him. "Is your father a rich man?" he asked.

"No, sir, we are very poor," answered Pinocchio.

"That is too bad. Well, take these six gold coins to him and tell him he has a brave son."

With many thanks Pinocchio bid good-bye to Fire-Eater. He embraced all the players and then set out for home.

He had not gone more than a mile when he met a lame Fox and a blind Cat. The Fox led the Cat and the Cat allowed the Fox to lean on him like a crutch.

"Good day to you, Pinocchio," said the Fox as the puppet passed.

"How do you know my name?" Pinocchio asked, puzzled.

"I know your father very well," replied the Fox.

"When did you see him last?"

"Only yesterday. He was out walking in the village without a coat to shield him from the snowy day."

"Well, he won't be without a coat much longer," Pinocchio said proudly.

"How will you, the son of a poor carpenter, manage that?" the Fox asked, as he moved closer to Pinocchio and put one arm around the puppet's shoulder. As he did so, the Cat covered his mouth with his paw to stifle a laugh. But Pinocchio noticed the Cat anyway. To prove that his remarks were nothing to laugh at, he pulled from his pocket the sparkling gold coins Fire-Eater had given him just hours earlier, saying, "Don't laugh at me. I am quite rich enough to buy my father a coat."

"Rich, indeed!" the Fox exclaimed, staring at the gold coins glistening in the sunlight. He could barely contain his greed and even his supposedly lame leg began to straighten. As for the blind Cat, when he heard the musical clinking of the coins, he immediately opened his sharp green eyes to get a better look. But both the Cat and the Fox returned to their pathetic condition before Pinocchio noticed. If he had, things might have gone differently for him.

"Pinocchio, you are extraordinarily lucky to have met us this morning," the Fox announced, as he slapped the puppet on the back. "What else will you do with your small fortune?"

"I must buy myself another school book, so I can go to school."

"Oh, dear," the Fox said to the Cat. "It is fortunate that our friend Pinocchio has met us." The Cat meowed in solemn agreement.

"Going back to school would be a mistake, Pinocchio. It was my own thirst for study that resulted in my lame leg, and my poor friend the Cat has gone blind from reading too many books. You can see that study is a dangerous thing indeed."

Just then a Bluebird flew overhead and landed on a nearby tree. "Beware, Pinocchio, don't take advice from fools or you will be one yourself."

Suddenly the Cat sprang up, caught the bird, and stuffed him in his mouth, feathers and all.

"Oh, the poor bird. Why did you do that?" asked Pinocchio.

"That was to teach him a lesson. Next time he will think twice before he attempts to insult gentlemen," the Fox said. "Indeed, birds have absolutely no respect at all for gentlemen, none at all. But as I was saying, Pinocchio, it is lucky we have met, because we know a way that you can turn your few coins into thousands! Would you like that, my friend?"

"Thousands! Of course, but how?" asked Pinocchio.

"Don't you worry about that. Just come along with us. We

must not waste a minute." The Fox took Pinocchio's arm and began to lead him away.

"Where are we going?"

"To the Owl Country."

"No, I can't go. I must go home. My father is waiting for me. I'm sure he is worried. I promised to go to school, but instead I went to a puppet show and then I almost got burned up. Ooh! I can still feel the heat from those terrible flames—"

"Yes, yes, my handsome wooden head, this is all very interesting, but fortunes are made and lost in a matter of a day. One must be quick to not lose one's chance," the Fox cut in before Pinocchio could finish.

"Lose a fortune. Lose one's chance," the Cat muttered in agreement.

"Yes, it's a shame. If you must go, then you must, but remember, Pinocchio, you are losing the chance to turn those five coins into a fortune. Think what your father could do with all that wealth. He could gladly wait for you a little longer if he only knew," the Fox continued.

"If he only knew," repeated the Cat.

"Just think of it, Pinocchio, tomorrow you'll have turned your gold coins to a thousand!" the Fox exclaimed.

"Gold coins," echoed the Cat.

"But how is this possible?" asked Pinocchio.

"All right, I will tell you. In Owl Country there is a magic piece of land called the Promise Field. If you bury your gold coins there with a few drops of water and then go away for just a short time, when you return you'll find that a tree has sprouted in that very spot. But this is no ordinary tree, for it will have bloomed clusters of gold coins like grapes on a vine! All that is left for you to do is pull them down and return home a wealthy boy," the Fox said.

"Bunches of golden grapes!" said the Cat.

The Fox gave the Cat a strong shove with his withered leg. "No! Not grapes, but *gold coins!* More than anyone could ever ask for."

"How wonderful! Could we go now? And for your kindness I will gladly give you a gift for helping me," said Pinocchio.

"Don't insult us!" the Fox replied. "We are gentlemen, remember. The only reward my friend the noble Cat and myself wish is the joy of seeing you prosper. We have no need of money ourselves. That you would even consider giving us money is offensive to us."

"The joy of money!" shouted the Cat.

"Be still!" said the Fox, as he knocked the Cat to the ground. Again, he took Pinocchio's arm. "We will go at once, but first we must help our poor blind friend for he seems to have fallen."

CHAPTER XI

After picking up the Cat and dusting him off, they proceeded on their way. They walked for miles, and toward evening they came to the Tavern of the Red Lobster.

"My friend, we are all weary from our long journey. Let us stop here to rest and have a light supper," the Fox suggested.

The Innkeeper welcomed them and made the travelers comfortable at a table before the fireplace. The Cat said he had an upset stomach and would order a small meal of thirty-five mullets in tomato sauce and then four portions of tripe with cheese and butter. After devouring this he had four more portions with butter and cheese and then said he couldn't eat another bite. But since lobster was the specialty of the inn, he felt it would be a shame not to sample a few. So he ordered ten lobsters in hot sauce, and with a little effort managed to finish every one. The Fox said his doctor had put him on a diet and that it was always unwise to eat too heavy a meal before bedtime. So he ordered stewed hare dressed with a dozen young tender chickens and roosters. As a finishing course he had a plate of some partridge, a few pheasants, a couple of rabbits, and twelve toads, with lizards and grapes. Pinocchio had advanced indigestion from daydreams of gold coins, so he had a handful of walnuts and a crust of bread. When they finished their meal they asked for two good rooms and decided to sleep until midnight, when they would resume their journey.

Pinocchio fell asleep almost immediately and dreamed of a beautiful tree with its branches weighted down with gold coins. As the breeze blew through the branches he heard the coins whisper, "Those who want us must come get us."

He woke with a start. The Innkeeper was knocking at his door. "Your companions have been called away. It seems the Cat's mother has become suddenly sick. However, they left in such a hurry they failed to pay their bill," said the Innkeeper.

"That is too bad," said Pinocchio. He gave the Innkeeper one gold coin in payment and hurried out into the night to find the Promise Field on his own.

It was very dark. As he walked bats flew swiftly by, flapping their wings against his long nose. He cried out, not knowing what they were. Then he heard a familiar voice and before his eyes he saw the ghost of the talking Cricket. "Pinocchio, go back home at once," the Cricket said in a far-off voice that seemed to come from the depths of a grave.

"I must go on. Tomorrow I will be rich," Pinocchio replied.

"It is very late and very dangerous to be out. Take what you have left of your gold coins and go home to your father. He is brokenhearted because he thinks you are lost."

"No. Tomorrow my father will be rich. I must go on," Pinocchio insisted.

"Pinocchio, don't trust anyone who promises to make you rich overnight," warned the Cricket.

"You are always ordering and advising. Go away, Cricket. I must go on."

"Then good night, Pinocchio, but I hope you will be safe from thieves tonight."

The Cricket vanished, his image disappearing like the snuffed-out flame of a candle. Then there was total darkness, and Pinocchio felt more alone than ever.

CHAPTER XII

How is a boy ever to get ahead in this world if others insist on frightening him? Everybody scolds me, everybody threatens me, everyone is always giving me advice, everyone wants to be my teacher. That worrisome Cricket is the worst of all. Just because I know something more about getting rich than he does, he tries to frighten me. He tries to scare me into thinking thieves will rob me. He tries to make me lose my courage. I think he tries to make up things to scare me just to keep me from doing things for myself. I'm not a baby. I'm not afraid. Suppose I do meet thieves. I know what I'll do. I'll walk right up to them and tell them not to bother me! I'll tell them to go away. When they hear that they will run for their lives because they will know I'm not afraid. Then when they run one way, I will run the other and that will be that!"

All the same, Pinocchio was frightened as he stumbled on into the blackness. He imagined he heard footsteps shuffling first behind him, then in front of him. But it was too dark for him to be sure. The wind howled through the trees, making a terrible sound. "Perhaps," he thought, "they aren't footsteps at all, but just the sounds of the night." He stopped to make sure he was on the right road. Suddenly, two cloaked figures sprang from the bushes. Pinocchio just had time enough to pop the gold coins into his mouth before the thieves grabbed him.

"Your money or your life," two gruff voices snarled.

Because of the coins in his mouth, Pinocchio was unable to reply. So instead, he bowed and shook his head, hoping the thieves would think he was only a poor wooden puppet who couldn't speak.

"Come on, out with it or we'll finish you and your father, too," the taller thief threatened.

"Finish you and your father, too," repeated the other.

"No, no, not my father," Pinocchio cried, and as he spoke the coins clinked.

"Aha! You've got them in your mouth. Open up or you're dead for sure."

Pinocchio refused, so the taller thief took him by his feet and turned him upside down. "Then we'll shake it out of you," he growled. At the same time the other thief tried to pry open Pinocchio's mouth with his paws. Quick as he could, Pinocchio bit the paw. The thief's screams startled his companion, and in the confusion Pinocchio twisted free. He jumped over the bushes and started to run, with the two thieves after him.

Pinocchio ran and ran till he saw a tree. He just managed to scramble up it before the thieves arrived. They tried to climb it, but their cloaks got in the way and they only slipped back down again. Pinocchio was sure he was safe. Yet his hopes were crushed when he saw the two thieves carry twigs to the tree and start a fire beneath it. In seconds, the tree was ablaze. Before Pinocchio could be cooked alive he jumped down and ran off, with the thieves in hot pursuit. As the sun began to rise Pinocchio came upon a ditch filled with muddy water. Summoning up all his strength, he leaped, clearing the ditch in one bound. The thieves tried to follow, but again their cloaks got in the way and they both landed in the mud. Pinocchio thought he had lost them at last, but when he turned back to be sure, he saw the two cloaked figures now caked with mud running behind him.

CHAPTER XIII

The poor puppet's legs ached from running all night, and he felt he could not go another step. Then, off in the distance, hidden in the forest, he saw a tiny cottage.

"If only I can go a bit farther, I know I'll be safe there," he thought.

At last he reached the door of the cottage. He knocked desperately, but there was no answer. Frantic, he knocked louder and kicked at the door. He could hear the thieves closing in on him. Pinocchio began to shout, "Help, help! Please let me in before I am killed."

Just then a window opened. To Pinocchio's surprise he saw there the beautiful face of a young girl. Her skin was the color of white wax candles and her bright-blue hair fell in long wavy ringlets down her slender shoulders. Her hands were folded across her chest. When she spoke her voice was faint and distant. "Go away. No one lives here anymore. Everyone is dead and gone to the grave."

"Please, beautiful one, let me in. You are not dead," pleaded Pinocchio.

But the window shut soundlessly. "Please, beautiful angel," the puppet cried, "let me in before it's too late. Have pity on a poor boy."

"Now you won't get away again!" the taller thief growled. And before Pinocchio could run, they had caught hold of him again.

"Give us your money at once!" they snarled. Terrified,

Pinocchio shook from head to toe. As he did so, the coins rattled under his tongue, but he would not open his mouth. At once the thieves took out knives as sharp as razors and slashed at his back. Fortunately the puppet was made of good hard wood. All that happened was that the thieves broke their knives.

"All right, then, there is nothing left but to hang you." They dragged Pinocchio to a large old oak tree. They bound his hands and feet and strung him up by the neck from a high, thick branch. Then they sat down on the grass to wait for Pinocchio to take his final breath. They waited and waited, but time passed and, to their mutual disgust, by afternoon, poor Pinocchio was still not dead. On the contrary, his eyes were still open and he was kicking harder than ever.

"This is a most disagreeable situation," said one of the thieves. "Since you are taking such a long time to die we will leave you here, but please do us the courtesy of being dead when we return tomorrow." With that he and the other left Pinocchio to die all alone.

Still more time passed and a strong wind began to blow. Pinocchio swung back and forth like a bell in a church steeple. He could hardly breathe.

"Father, if only you were here to help me," he cried softly. Then he heaved a heavy sigh and hung silent as death.

CHAPTER XIV

Nearby, the window of the tiny cottage opened and the head of the young girl peeked out. She saw the puppet hanging stiffly from the limb of the old oak tree, and she felt great pity for him. "Poor Pinocchio," she said, shaking her pretty head sadly. She clapped her hands and at once a large black Hawk flew to the window. "What is your wish, Blue Fairy?" asked the Hawk.

"Friend Hawk, fly to the great oak and with your strong beak cut the knot that is choking Pinocchio. Then lay him gently on the ground and return to me."

When the Hawk returned he said, "I have done what you asked."

"Tell me then, is he dead or alive?" asked the Fairy.

"He looks dead, but when I broke the knot I thought I heard him say he felt better," answered the Hawk.

The Fairy clapped her hands again. A dog who was dressed in finest coachman's livery walked on his hind legs into the room. He was a most impressive sight. He wore a three-cornered hat trimmed in gold thread over a handsome white powdered wig. His coat was deep dark chocolate velvet with real diamond buttons. His trousers were bright-red satin, and he wore pink silk stockings and yellow boots. The final touch was a blue satin umbrella hooked in his long tail to keep off the rain.

"Medoro, take the carriage from the stable and quickly

fetch Pinocchio, who is at the foot of the great oak tree."

Medoro set off immediately in a brilliant blue carriage drawn by a hundred well-groomed white mice. He lifted Pinocchio gently and placed him on the tufted canary-feathered seat in the carriage, then drove directly back to the Blue Fairy. She took Pinocchio into her arms and carried him to a bed made of diamonds and pearls. At once she called the most famous doctors she knew. When they arrived there was a Crow, an Owl, and a talking Cricket.

"Good doctors, please examine Pinocchio and tell me if he is dead or alive," requested the Fairy.

After looking Pinocchio over, the Crow spoke first. "It is my expert opinion that this puppet is dead. However, if I am wrong, then he is most certainly alive."

"I see," said the Fairy.

Then it was the Owl's turn to speak. "I must respectfully disagree with my learned colleague's diagnosis. It is my professional belief that this puppet Pinocchio is alive, but even *I* am not often right and I'm afraid I seem to have forgotten my glasses in my haste to arrive quickly. So perhaps it would be safer to say that there is no doubt that he is quite dead."

The talking Cricket spoke last. "If the Fairy does not mind, I choose not to speak of this case, which is certainly a difficult one indeed." Without taking a breath he continued,

"This very puppet is familiar to me. I have known him for some time, and for this reason I wish to say not another word and wait for further developments."

Pinocchio, who had not moved until then, now gave a twitch that shook the entire bed.

Without being urged, the Cricket continued. "But if the Fairy were to insist, I would only add that this puppet is a terrible rascal and a fool who does not know good advice from bad."

Pinocchio slipped under the sheets and tried to hide.

"Furthermore, if anyone cares to know, I am sure that this very day his father is nursing a broken heart over this worthless toothpick!"

The sound of weeping came from under the bedcovers. When the Fairy lifted them, she discovered Pinocchio crying.

"Ah, you see, when a dead boy cries it is a sure sign that he is getting well!" said the Crow.

"Again it saddens me to disagree with my esteemed colleague," said the Owl, "but in my opinion when a live boy cries it is a sure sign that he'd rather be dead."

CHAPTER XV

The Fairy thanked the three doctors, and when they were on their way she returned to Pinocchio holding a glass of

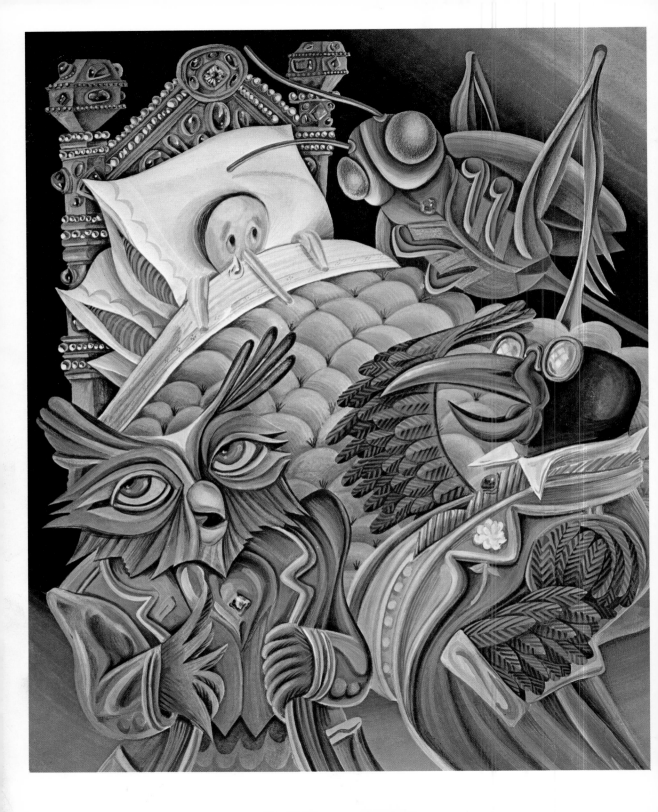

water mixed with some medicine.

"Drink this, child, and before long you will be better," she said.

"I don't like medicine. It's too bitter," he said, pouting.

"That is true, but it will do you good."

Still Pinocchio refused.

"If you will drink it, I will give you some candy to chase away the bitter taste," the Fairy said to persuade him.

"If you give me the candy first, I will take the medicine," said Pinocchio.

"Do you promise?" asked the Fairy.

Pinocchio promised. He ate the candy in one gulp, licked his fingers, and said, "If medicine tasted like candy, I'd gladly eat it every day."

"Now keep your promise and drink your medicine," said the Fairy.

Pinocchio took the glass from her but refused to drink. He wrinkled his nose and said, "No, it's too bitter."

"You haven't even tasted it. How can you be sure?" the Fairy reasoned patiently.

"I can smell it. Give me another piece of candy and I'll wash it down with the medicine."

"Very well," the Fairy said, giving Pinocchio another piece.

"It's no use. I can't do it," Pinocchio said, but only after he finished the second piece of candy.

"Why not?" asked the Fairy.

"I need another piece of candy."

"No!" the Fairy said resolutely. "Keep your promise and at least try to drink the medicine."

Pinocchio made another attempt, but paused again.

"I can't drink it."

"What's wrong now?" she asked.

"My pillows are mussed," he whined.

The Fairy arranged his pillows neatly. "Come now, no more excuses. Take your medicine and you'll feel better."

"No, honestly it's no use. I can't do it."

"Pinocchio, you'll die of fever if you don't drink it."

"I don't care. I'd rather die than drink this awful stuff. The taste alone will kill me."

"Very well then," said the Fairy. She clapped her hands and the bedroom door opened. Four black Rabbits walked into the room. They were dressed entirely in black and on their shoulders they carried a small coffin.

"What's this?" Pinocchio asked, as he sat up to get a better look.

"We've come to take you away," the Rabbits said in unison.

"But I'm not dead yet!" Pinocchio insisted.

"You will be soon, since you refuse to take your medicine. So let's go," the Rabbits said firmly.

"Fairy! Send them away. Here, look, I'll drink my medicine," Pinocchio said, and he drank it down in one big swallow.

"So, we've come for nothing," the Rabbits said, annoyed, and they turned to go, carrying the coffin with them.

Almost immediately Pinocchio felt better, and he was able to get out of bed.

"So, you are feeling better," said the Fairy.

"That was a close call with death. If I ever again must drink medicine, I will remember the black Rabbits," Pinocchio said.

The Fairy asked Pinocchio how he had come to the forest and why he had been chased by robbers. He told her his story, but left out the present whereabouts of the gold coins.

"Do you still have the gold coins?" asked the Fairy.

"No, I lost them," said Pinocchio. But it was a lie—he had the five coins hidden in his pocket.

"Tell me, how did you lose them?" she asked.

"I don't remember," Pinocchio lied. At this second lie his long nose began to grow. "Oh, now I remember," he said hesitantly. "I swallowed them when I drank the medicine." The puppet's nose went on growing, and the Fairy began to laugh. Pinocchio was so embarrassed he tried to run, but his nose was so long that he couldn't get out the door.

CHAPTER XVI

Pinocchio began to cry. He apologized to the Fairy and admitted that he still had the gold coins safely in his pocket. Then Fairy clapped her hands and a flock of woodpeckers flew into the room. They landed on Pinocchio's nose and began to peck away at it. Soon they had reduced it to a more normal size.

"Thank you," Pinocchio said, as he wiped the tears from his eyes.

"Now what shall we do while we wait for your father to arrive?" asked the Fairy.

"My father?" asked Pinocchio.

"Yes, it's all arranged. I have sent for your father. He will be here soon and then, if you like, you will both live here with me."

Pinocchio was so delighted that he put his arms around the Fairy and gave her a big kiss. Then he went outside to watch for Geppetto's arrival. He walked up the hill and stood by the old oak tree. Suddenly, who should appear but the Fox and the Cat. They seemed very startled to see their good friend Pinocchio.

"Goodness, we were so worried about you," the Fox said, once he had recovered from his surprise.

Pinocchio told them everything that had happened since he had seen them last. Both the Fox and the Cat seemed to find the whole story fascinating. As they talked, Pinocchio noticed the Cat had lost one of his paws. He tried to explain, but he could only stutter. The Fox interrupted. "Our friend the Cat is too shy to tell you that his generous nature forced him to give his paw to a poor starving wolf," the Fox said, as he gently patted the Cat's head.

"Tell us, Pinocchio, do you still have your gold coins?" inquired the Fox.

Pinocchio told them that he did indeed, except for the one he spent at the Tavern of the Red Lobster. "Well, it's not too late to plant them in the Promise Field," suggested the Fox.

"Another time, perhaps. Right now I am waiting here for my father."

"Another time and you might not have the chance," insisted the Fox. "The land has just been purchased by a greedy group who soon will have signs up to keep all good people out."

"Is it very far away?" Pinocchio asked, as he tried to make up his mind.

"Not far at all! If we left now you'd be back in plenty of time to meet your father," the Fox assured him. Pinocchio hesitated, but the Fox talked on and on until all the puppet could think of was his dream of the beautiful tree filled with gold coins.

"Let's go. I'm ready, but we must be back soon," Pinocchio said finally.

The three walked on till late in the day. At last they approached the entrance to a city. Beside the gate a sign read: FOOL'S TRAP. Since Pinocchio could not read, he paid no attention to the warning. Within the city Pinocchio saw starving dogs, sheep without fleece shivering in the cold, chickens without feathers, butterflies crawling on the ground without wings, and peacocks whose tails had been cut off walking with their heads bent in shame.

"Pay no attention to these fools," the Fox advised, as he hurried Pinocchio along.

Now and then a rich carriage rode by carrying a Fox, or a Cat, or a Vulture dressed in the height of fashion. On the other side of the city the travelers arrived at a barren field.

"Here we are," announced the Fox.

At once Pinocchio began to dig a hole just where the Fox instructed. Then he placed his five gold coins in the dry ground. He took some water from a nearly empty well, poured it over his small fortune, and covered it over with the dirt.

"Should I do anything else?" asked the puppet.

"No, my dear lucky friend, you have done everything

necessary. Now we must be on our way. As for you, go away for a while, and when you return you will see what you have harvested," said the Fox.

They shook hands and said good-bye. Pinocchio again promised them a gift, which they adamantly refused.

CHAPTER XVII

Filled with plans for his future riches, Pinocchio walked through the city. When he felt enough time had passed, he hurried back to the field. He expected to see a wonderful tree filled with gold, but the field was just as barren as before. Certain he had misjudged the spot, he walked the entire field. Nothing. He spun around and around looking in every direction till he was dizzy. Then he sat down on the ground and rested his head in his hands. Above him he heard a laugh. He looked up. In the branches of a dead tree he saw a Parrot. The Parrot was cleaning his few feathers as he laughed.

"Why are you laughing?" asked Pinocchio.

"No real reason. I tickle myself as I clean my feathers," the Parrot answered, as he ran a thin feather through his beak.

Pinocchio decided to ignore the Parrot. He went back to the well and returned with a bit more water, which he poured over the spot where he had planted his coins. Again he heard the Parrot's laughter.

"What is it now?" Pinocchio asked angrily.

"I'm laughing at a fool who believes every false tale he hears," replied the Parrot.

"Do you mean me?" demanded Pinocchio.

"Yes, I do. You were a fool to believe that gold could grow on trees like flowers. Once I was as foolish, and now it is too late for either of us. So one might as well laugh."

"I don't understand you," the puppet said, confused.

"All right, I'll explain it to you. When you went away the Fox and the Cat came back in a flash, dug up your coins, and ran off."

When Pinocchio heard this he began digging frantically. He dug a hole big enough for himself, but he did not find his coins. Then he got up, dusted himself off, and with as much self-respect as he could muster he walked toward the city courthouse to make a complaint.

When Pinocchio arrived at the courthouse he found the judge was a Gorilla. He sat at his desk wearing a black robe, and in his hand he held a gavel that he pounded on the desk to keep order in the crowded courtroom. Each time he struck the desk his glasses slid down his nose and his dignified white wig came forward over his eyes. The courtroom was a mass of confusion, with angry people shouting complaints of all kinds. Patiently Pinocchio waited his turn, and at last he was called. The judge listened as the puppet told his story. When he was finished the judge looked at him sternly, saying nothing. Then: "Hmmm, yes, I see it's an open-and-shut case." He hit the desk with his gavel and called two large Dogs dressed as Policemen into the room. The judge pointed to Pinocchio and said, "Here is another fool who has been robbed of his money. Take him to jail at once."

Pinocchio began to protest, but the Policemen wasted no time. They handcuffed him and led him away to prison.

Four long months dragged by while Pinocchio remained locked in jail. Then one day the mayor of the city declared a holiday. There were festivities of all kinds and all the criminals were set free. As Pinocchio prepared to leave, the jailer stopped him. "Just a minute, you are not a criminal," he said.

"Are only criminals to be freed today?" asked Pinocchio.

"That's right," answered the jailer.

"Well, I'm the worst of them all," said the puppet.

"Oh, in that case, out you go," said the jailer.

CHAPTER XVIII

When Pinocchio left the prison he didn't stop to look back. He ran as fast as he could till he was out of the city. More than anything, he wanted to get back to the Fairy and his father. The roads were very muddy and as he ran he was splashed with mud from head to toe. Sometimes he even sank down into the mud almost to his knees. But the puppet was too busy thinking of the wonderful welcome he would receive once he got to the Fairy's house to let the mud bother him.

But suddenly he stopped in his tracks, terrified, for an enormous slimy green Serpent lay stretched out along the road, making it impossible for him to pass. The Serpent's amber eyes glowed like fire, and the point of his long tail had a trail of smoke puffing from it. Pinocchio was so frightened that he turned back and hid behind a tree to wait for the Serpent to go on his way. Time passed, but whenever Pinocchio peeked out to see if the road was clear, the Serpent remained, and the puppet could see the flash of his eyes and the curl of smoke from his tail.

Finally, Pinocchio decided he must be brave. He walked straight up to the Serpent and said in a polite voice, "Excuse me, Mr. Serpent, but would you be so kind as to move aside so I may pass?"

The Serpent appeared not to have heard him at all and became ever so still. So once more Pinocchio began, "You see, I must be on my way. My father is waiting for me. So you must let me pass."

Still no answer came from the Serpent. In fact, the Serpent seemed to be asleep or dead, for his eyes were shut and his tail had ceased smoking.

"Are you dead?" asked the puppet hopefully.

Without any further hesitation, he started to raise one leg

over the creature. But just then, the Serpent sprang up violently, throwing the puppet head over heels backward into the deep mud. Pinocchio's head was stuck in the mud while he wiggled his feet wildly to right himself. The Serpent laughed so heartily and long at the ridiculous sight of the squirming puppet that he finally burst an artery and died instantly.

Eventually Pinocchio freed himself from the mud and began to run along the road, hoping to reach the Fairy's house before dark. Along the way he passed a vineyard, and there he stopped to rest. He slept for a while, and when he woke he was very hungry. On the side of the fence that enclosed the vineyard he saw some beautifully ripened purple grapes hanging on the vine. Pinocchio climbed over the fence and reached for some low-hanging grapes. Suddenly with a CRACK! he felt his legs seized by the iron teeth of a trap. He cried out in pain, but there was no one to hear him.

Time passed and night closed in. Pinocchio's legs ached terribly and the darkness frightened him. "Is there no one to help me?" he cried.

Just then he saw a small spot of blue light. It was a tiny Firefly. "You poor child, how did you manage to fall into this trap?" she asked.

"I was only trying to pick a few grapes," Pinocchio whimpered.

"Were the grapes yours to pick?" the Firefly asked.

"No," the puppet answered unhappily.

"Then you had no business picking them," she replied.

Just then their conversation was interrupted by the sound of footsteps. It was the Farmer who owned the vineyard. "So I have finally caught something in my trap," he said.

He raised his lantern and looked at his captive. "You little robber. I'll see to it that you steal no more of my chickens."

"No, no, it isn't true. I only tried to eat a few grapes," said Pinocchio.

"Chickens or grapes, it makes little difference. A thief who steals grapes will most likely steal chickens," the Farmer said. Then he opened the trap, took Pinocchio by the neck, and carried him to his house. "I'm going to teach you a lesson. This morning my faithful dog died and now there is no one to watch my chickens. For your punishment you will take his place. And my chickens had better all be here tomorrow or you will be sorry," the Farmer said sternly.

He took the dog's collar and clamped it tightly around Pinocchio's neck. Then he went to bed and left Pinocchio out in the rain. Pinocchio crawled into the doghouse, shaking his head. "I am the most foolish puppet that has ever lived."

Before long Pinocchio heard scuffling and whispers. He stuck his head out of the doghouse and saw four Weasels slowly approaching. The leader came forward. "Hello, Melampo, is that you?" he asked.

"I'm not Melampo. I am Pinocchio," answered the puppet.

"Where is Melampo, and what are you doing here?" asked the leader.

"The old dog died this morning, and I have taken his place," answered Pinocchio.

"That's too bad, he was a fine dog indeed. Now let us see if you are also a fine dog," the Weasel said.

"Excuse me! I'm not a dog, I'm a puppet," Pinocchio said.

"I see. All the same, we would like to offer you the bargain we had with the former tenant here. We will gladly give you one chicken in exchange for your keeping silent while we take some for ourselves," said the Weasel.

"And this is the arrangement you had with Melampo?" asked Pinocchio.

"Exactly! It worked out very well for everyone. Now, be a nice dog—oh, a thousand pardons!—a nice puppet, and rest quietly. We will return with a lovely fat chicken for your breakfast," the Weasel said. Then he led his small troop to the chicken house. No sooner had they slipped inside than Pinocchio slammed the door shut and bolted it. Then he yelled for the Farmer. The man jumped out of bed and rushed from his house, stopping only to get his rifle.

"Well?" asked the Farmer.

"The thieves are locked in the hen house," said Pinocchio.

In no time, the Farmer had all four Weasels safely tucked up in a sack.

"These creatures will make a fine coat for someone," he said with satisfaction.

Pinocchio kept silent about Melampo. "Let the old dog lie in peace," he thought. "It will do no good to accuse him now. After all, the dead are dead, and the best thing to do is leave them to their dreams."

"Good boy, Pinocchio," said the Farmer. "I will give you your freedom as a reward for your help.

CHAPTER XIX

Pinocchio left immediately for the Fairy's cottage. When he arrived he saw the old oak tree on the hill and he saw the very spot where he had met the Fox and the Cat, but the cottage had disappeared. Instead, he found a slab of stone in its place. On it were these words:

HERE LIES THE FAIRY
WITH THE BLUE HAIR. SHE DIED GRIEVING
FOR HER MISSING BROTHER,
PINOCCHIO.

Though Pinocchio could not read, a chill came over him so that he sensed what the words meant. He dropped to his knees and began to weep. He stayed at the stone for hours. In the morning, with nothing left to do, he walked on, but he had nowhere to go. Aimlessly he looked around and saw above him a Dove with pale-blue feathers flying low. When the Dove saw Pinocchio he flew down. He was as large as a peacock.

"Excuse me, young fellow," the Dove said. "Do you happen to know where I might find a puppet named Pinocchio?"

"Pinocchio? I'm Pinocchio!" said the puppet.

"Oh, how very fortunate. Then you must know a carpenter by the name of Geppetto," continued the Dove.

"Yes, of course, he is my father. Please tell me, do you know where I can find him?"

"I do. I saw him three days ago. He was preparing to sail off on a little raft with the hope of finding you in some faraway land," the Dove replied.

"How long will it take me to catch up to him?"

"It's a long distance. I will gladly take you, if you like," said the Dove.

"Yes, please," Pinocchio said eagerly.

"Very good, then climb on my back and off we'll go."

The Dove glided gently toward the clouds. It was a beautiful morning, and Pinocchio felt dizzy with excitement.

"Don't look down, and hold tight," advised the Dove.

They flew on together till night.

"Are you hungry?" asked the Dove.

"Yes, but I will not mind waiting unless you wish to stop," said Pinocchio.

"You really *are* anxious to see your father, Pinocchio. It seems you are changing your habits," the Dove observed.

Soon they passed an empty pigeon coop, where they decided to stop and rest. There they found a pan of water and a plate of dried seeds.

"Well, this is fine for me, but I'm afraid there is nothing else to offer you, Pinocchio," said the Dove.

Pinocchio never even thought to complain. "I don't mind. Help yourself. Whatever is left will be enough for me."

These were the first seeds the puppet had ever eaten, but that night he felt certain there couldn't possibly be anything that tasted better. After their meal they set out again, flying all the rest of the night. At daybreak they arrived at the edge of the sea.

The tide was coming in, and white foamy waves curled in toward the shoreline. A group of people stood near the shore. In the deep waters they could see someone on a raft having trouble keeping afloat. After Pinocchio and the Dove landed, the puppet walked over to the crowd.

"What's going on out there?" he asked.

One Fisherman answered, "That man on the raft looks as though he's done for."

Pinocchio was filled with a sense of dread. "Do you know who he is?"

"He's the carpenter, Geppetto. The poor man sailed off today to find his son," the Fisherman answered.

"Father!" Pinocchio shouted, but Geppetto couldn't hear him. As they watched they saw the little raft, engulfed by waves, disappear from sight.

"Poor old man, there is no hope for him now," said the Fisherman.

Without a thought for himself, Pinocchio jumped into the water, and called out, "Don't worry, Father, I'll save you."

As the crowd watched, Pinocchio vanished.

"Brave boy, but I'm afraid its hopeless," the Fisherman said.

CHAPTER XX

Pinocchio was a remarkable swimmer. His small wooden body aided him in keeping afloat as the angry waves crashed down and tossed him violently. He swam on endlessly, thinking only of saving his father, but there was no sign of Geppetto.

The next morning, Pinocchio saw a thin line of islands far off in the distance. He swam toward them wearily. As he got closer, a huge wave rose up and lifted him. It struck the sandy shoreline and threw the helpless puppet onto the beach. The force of the wave would have killed an ordinary boy, but Pinocchio, though dazed at first, was unharmed.

"I guess I should consider myself lucky to be alive. Thank you, wave, for giving me a ride."

Now that he was safely on the beach, he scanned the waters for any trace of the tiny raft and Geppetto. He saw nothing. The sea was surprisingly calm.

"Perhaps my father was fortunate enough to be washed up here, too."

But as he looked up and down the beach, his hopes sank. There was no evidence that he was right. Just then a large blue-green Fish swam over to him.

"Hello, Pinocchio," said the Fish.

"Hello, Mr. Fish. Tell me, have you seen a man on a raft in these waters today?" asked Pinocchio.

"Who is the man?" asked the Fish.

"His name is Geppetto. He sailed out to sea yesterday to search for his worthless son."

"No, I haven't seen him. But if he was out yesterday, I'm afraid that the terrible Dogfish has swallowed him."

"Is he big enough to swallow a man?" Pinocchio asked.

"I should say so! Big enough. He's as big as a five-story house and fierce as a dragon. No one is safe when he swims nearby, and he was out here yesterday," the Fish answered.

"Oh, my poor father!" said Pinocchio as he began to cry.

"What will you do now?"

"I don't know. Is there a town nearby?" the puppet asked.

"If you follow that road to the left, you will come to the Town of the Do-Bees."

Pinocchio thanked the Fish and started on his way. Now and then he turned back to catch a glimpse of the sea. When it was finally out of view, he said to himself sadly, "I suppose there is nothing more I can do. My father is lost forever. I must make my own way alone in the world."

The Town of the Do-Bees buzzed with activity. Everywhere Pinocchio looked he saw people intent on their work.

"This isn't my sort of place. Doesn't anyone relax and just do nothing? These people make me tired just looking at them."

Pinocchio was hungry. He thought perhaps he could beg for money for food. The first person he asked was a Stonemason who was meticulously laying brick for a wall.

"Excuse me, sir, could you give some money for food to a hungry boy?" he asked.

"I'm sorry, but I don't give away money for nothing. If you

can lay brick, you can work for your food," the Stonemason replied without interrupting his work.

"No, that would make me too tired," said the puppet.

The next man he saw was pulling a cart filled with coal.

"Pardon me, sir, could you spare some money to a poor, starving boy?"

"I will gladly give you some money, if you will pull my cart," answered the man.

But Pinocchio shook his head. "Pulling a cart is business for a donkey!"

The man laughed and said, "Then satisfy your hunger by eating two slices of your pride spread with a large portion of your laziness. I hope that fills your stomach."

Pinocchio walked off in a huff. "People in this town are not very generous."

But soon after he saw a Shopkeeper sitting at his desk. "Good sir, could you give me some money for food?" Pinocchio asked.

"I have no money for beggars, my boy. If you can count out sums for me, I will gladly pay you for your work."

"No, I don't know how to count," answered the puppet.

"Don't they teach children anything in school these days?" asked the Shopkeeper.

"I haven't gone to school yet," explained Pinocchio.

"Well, go to school and learn, my boy, then come back and I will give you a good job."

Disappointed, Pinocchio walked out of the shop. All the rest of the day it was the same. No one would give money to a boy who was too lazy to work. Finally he saw a young woman. She was dressed in blue with a blue scarf tied around her head. In both hands she carried two heavy pails filled with water.

"I'm so thirsty. May I have a drink of water?" asked Pinocchio.

"Certainly you may," said the woman.

Pinocchio drank his fill and said, "If only it was as easy to get food."

"If you will carry my pails home for me, I will give you some bread I baked this morning."

Pinocchio didn't answer. The woman continued. "I could add some home-churned butter." Still the puppet did not reply. "I have orange marmalade to sweeten it," she said.

At last Pinocchio could not resist. "Those pails look very heavy, but let me carry them for you all the same," he said as he took the pails. They were very heavy indeed, but the thought of something to eat helped him struggle up the hill.

When they arrived, the woman took the tired puppet into her kitchen. She spread out a checkered tablecloth and set before him two thick slices of fragrant fresh bread, rich butter, and sweet orange marmalade. Pinocchio finished every bite and felt revived.

"You remind me of someone, but she was just a girl," said Pinocchio.

"Really? And did you like her very much?" asked the woman with a smile.

"I loved her with all my heart," said Pinocchio.

"Then why did you leave her?" inquired the woman.

"I didn't!" the puppet shouted, and tears filled his eyes. Just then, he stopped and looked more closely at the woman.

"Wait!" he said, as she turned her head away from him.

"It *is* you! I know it's you! You have the same face as she and your hair is blue," he said excitedly.

"What do you mean?" she said, adjusting her scarf. "How do you know?"

"But it is you, Blue Fairy. Tell me how have you grown up so quickly," Pinocchio asked, taking her hand in his.

"Time has passed, Pinocchio. You have been gone a long while. It is you who have not changed," said the Blue Fairy.

Then the puppet told her how he had trusted the Fox and the Cat again and how they had betrayed him, and about his months in jail and all the rest.

"I tried to find you. I came back and saw the cottage was gone. I was sure I had lost you forever."

"You needn't fear any longer, Pinocchio. If you will promise me never to play the foolish puppet again, we will always be together."

"But tell me how I can grow quickly just like you?" he begged.

"You can't grow. You are a puppet. Only boys grow up," said the Fairy.

"Then how do I become a real boy?"

"Wooden boys only become real boys if they deserve it."

"Please tell me what to do and I will do it."

"Well, they do all the things you have refused to do. You can't be interested in knowing," the Fairy said doubtfully.

"You're wrong. Please tell me—I'll do anything!" Pinocchio begged.

"Things like working hard and studying in school. Good boys aren't selfish. They tell the truth."

"I see," said Pinocchio sadly. "Everything I've done is the opposite of that. I like to run and play instead of work and go to school. I don't always mind you, do I?" he asked.

The Fairy shook her head gravely.

"And I don't often tell the truth, either," said Pinocchio. "But I want to do better, really I do," he added earnestly.

"Do you promise me, Pinocchio?"

"I promise. And I want to help my father. Do you know where he is?"

"I can't say."

"Can you tell me if I will see him again?"

"I think you will."

"Then there is a chance!" Pinocchio said happily. "I promise I'll be good, you'll see. Tell me what I must do."

"You must begin school tomorrow morning," she said.

Pinocchio's spirits dimmed a bit.

"Then you will learn a trade," she continued.

Pinocchio became very serious. He squinted his eyes and began mumbling to himself.

"What are you mumbling, Pinocchio?"

"I'm thinking maybe it's too late for all this."

"That's ridiculous. It's never too late if you want to enough," said the Fairy, smiling.

Pinocchio heaved a deep sigh. "Well, it isn't going to be easy for me. I'd rather do nothing even now."

"Pinocchio, remember you must not go back on your promise to me or you will never grow!"

"I will try. I'll remember my promise, but I can see it won't be easy to change my nature."

"It is never easy to change one's patterns, but your true nature is a good one, and I know you can change if you try."

CHAPTER XXI

Pinocchio didn't find school easy. At first the children made fun of him because he was a puppet. They stole his hat, took his pencils, and knocked his books from his desk when the teacher wasn't looking. Finally he could stand it no longer.

"I've not come to school to be made a fool of," he said to them, but they only laughed the more. The leader of the group tried to pull Pinocchio's nose. But the boy wasn't fast enough. Pinocchio suddenly put out his foot and gave the boy a hard kick on the knee.

"Ouch! What hard feet," groaned the bully.

"And what sharp elbows!" said another who had tried to sneak behind the puppet, but instead got an elbow in his ribs.

After Pinocchio had defended himself, the teasing soon ended. The other children grew to respect him and made him their favorite in class.

He studied hard and his teacher praised his work. His only fault was that among his closest friends were boys who never worked and often got into trouble. Both the Fairy and his teacher warned him against these boys, but Pinocchio was confident he'd learned his lesson. So he would shrug his shoulders and tap his wooden head, saying proudly, "Now I have too much sense to ever get in trouble again."

One day, though, these friends called Pinocchio as he was walking to school.

"Pinocchio, have you heard the news? The great Dogfish has been washed up on the beach. We're going to see him. Do you want to come along?"

Pinocchio knew he should go to school, but the thought that this might be the very same giant fish that had swallowed Geppetto made it too great a temptation to refuse. He followed his friends down to the beach, but when they arrived there was no sign of the Dogfish.

"Where is he?" asked the puppet, as he scanned the length of the beach. "Where could he be?"

The boys began to laugh. "Maybe he went off for lunch," said one.

"Or maybe he's gone home for a nap," said another.

Pinocchio realized they had played a joke on him. "Why did you lie to me?" he asked.

"Because you're too good, Pinocchio."

"You work hard."

"You always have your lessons prepared."

"You never miss a day of school."

"And you make us look bad because of it," they all shouted.

"What do you want me to do, then?" asked Pinocchio.

"Be like us and forget school and lessons for a change," they demanded.

Then it was Pinocchio's turn to laugh. "I'll never do that."

The boys became angry. They pushed Pinocchio and tried to take his books. Though there were four against him, Pinocchio put up a good fight. When a boy picked up a heavy book to throw at Pinocchio, the puppet ducked just in time. The book missed him, but it hit another boy, who fell down and didn't stir.

"Is he dead?" asked Pinocchio.

But the others were too frightened to help. Instead, they all ran off, leaving Pinocchio to try to revive the fallen boy.

"Oh, please wake up," Pinocchio pleaded, but the boy did not move.

Just then two Policemen approached.

"What's going on here?" they asked.

"My schoolmate has been hurt," Pinocchio said, beginning to cry. "Please, can you help him?"

One of the Policemen lifted the boy up in his arms. The other picked up the book from the ground.

"Is this what struck him?" he asked sternly.

Pinocchio nodded.

The Policeman opened the book. There on the first page was written Pinocchio's name.

"Is this your book?"

Again Pinocchio nodded.

"Then you had better come to the police station for questioning, because you are under arrest."

"But I'm innocent!" Pinocchio protested.

"We will be the judge of that. Let's go," insisted the Policeman.

Pinocchio had no choice but to go with them. When they passed the Blue Fairy's cottage, Pinocchio hung his head in shame. The thought that she would soon hear what had happened filled him with sorrow.

At the door of the police station a strong gust of wind blew Pinocchio's hat from his head.

"Please, may I get my hat?" he asked.

"Go on," one of the Policemen said.

Pinocchio chased his hat as the wind swept it along the road. But when he finally caught it, he put it between his teeth and began to run toward the sea and away from the Police. They called after him, but Pinocchio would not stop. Then they let out their guard Dog, a strong and powerful mastiff, and ordered him to bring Pinocchio back.

CHAPTER XXII

It was a good race, but soon Pinocchio could feel the Dog's hot breath on his back. He knew if he faltered for a moment the Dog would have him between his teeth. Just a few feet away he saw the sparkling blue sea, and with one burst of strength the puppet leaped into the water. For a moment the Dog hesitated, then he too jumped in. But the Dog did not know how to swim as well as the puppet. Soon he panicked and began to splash frantically.

"Help! Help! I'm drowning," he pleaded.

Pinocchio, a safe distance away, tried not to notice. But the Dog's desperate cries were too much for him to ignore. He swam back to the drowning dog, grabbed his tail, and dragged him back to the beach. The poor Dog was so shaken he could barely stand up. Pinocchio turned from the Dog and swam out to sea again. He was not sure where he should go next. If he returned to the town, surely the police would not give up until they found him. Then too the idea of facing the disappointed Fairy was impossible for him. At last he decided he must go on. So he swam farther along, keeping close to shore in the hope of finding a safe place to stop. Eventually he saw a sandy beach and a cave. He swam for the shelter, hoping all the while that there he would have time to rest and dry himself. Suddenly he felt himself caught up in a net. Soon he was pulled from the water, trapped among dozens of squirming fish.

"Aha, a fine catch today," said the Fisherman, as he hauled the fish on board his boat.

"I'm not a fish," shouted Pinocchio.

But the Fisherman paid no attention. He carried the net filled with fish into his dark smokey cave. In one corner there was a roaring fire on which a pan filled with hot frying oil sat.

"Now let's see what fine fish we have," the Fisherman said to himself as he pushed his large flat hand into the net among mullets, whiting, sardines, sole, crabs, dear little anchovies, and the poor puppet. The Fisherman pulled out a huge fistful of lively fish. He drew them to his nose and sniffed.

"Haaa, fine fresh fish! Wonderful, wonderful," he said, throwing them into a tub filled with water. Over and over he did this until he finally had hold of Pinocchio. The Fisherman opened his large watery green eyes very wide and said, "What kind of fish is this?" as he tossed the unhappy puppet from one hand to the other. "Perhaps it is some sort of lobster."

"Lobster indeed!" shouted Pinocchio, insulted. "Be careful with me, you big walrus! Can't you see I'm a puppet?"

"A puppet fish. Hmmm, that's a new fish for me. This will be a rare delicacy for dinner tonight."

"*Dinner?* Don't you understand, I'm not a fish. I can talk just like you. Since when can an ordinary fish talk?"

"Beats me. It's obvious you are no ordinary fish. And to show proper respect I will let you decide how you shall be cooked."

"*What!*"

"Yes. As a token of my respect, I ask you, would you like to be dipped in a little flour and fried in oil, or would stewing perhaps be more agreeable to you? It's a little more trouble, but I don't mind. I'll even add a pan of fresh tomato sauce. What do you say?"

"To be perfectly honest, I'd much prefer to be set free."

"Don't be silly. I wouldn't dream of losing the chance to enjoy such a special puppet fish. Never mind, I understand it's a difficult decision. Allow me to choose for you. . . . I know! I think you would like to be fried with the other fish for company. Right?"

"You are hopeless," said Pinocchio. Then he began to cry and howl. "Let me go. Oh, if I had only gone to school today. Oh, oh, let me go."

He tried to break free from the Fisherman's strong grip, but it was no use. He was thrown into the tub of water with the rest of the fish. The Fisherman began to hum with delight. He took a plate and some white flour and dipped each fish into the flour and then dropped it into the smoking-hot frying oil. One by one they sizzled in the hot oil. At last Pinocchio's time came. The puppet could see death before him, and he froze with fear. The Fisherman had no mercy. He rolled the trembling Pinocchio in the flour until he looked just like a white puppet ghost. Finally the Fisherman took him to the hot frying oil. It looked like the end for Pinocchio, but just at that moment a large Dog came sniffing at the entrance to the cave.

CHAPTER XXIII

"Get out!" yelled the Fisherman as the Dog approached. But the Dog began to move closer. The animal was so hungry that the strong aroma of frying fish overcame any fear he might have had of the angry Fisherman.

"Get out, I say," repeated the Fisherman, moving as if to kick the Dog. This was foolish, because the Dog was very large and fierce and his hunger left him no patience for abuse. He bared his sharp teeth and gave a menacing growl.

Pinocchio, still in the hands of the Fisherman, parted his flour-coated lips and cried, "Please, someone save me."

The Dog, who by luck was the very mastiff Pinocchio had saved from drowning, recognized his friend immediately. He leaped up and snatched the puppet from the startled Fisherman. They were out of the cave in a flash. Furious, the Fisherman tried to chase after the Dog, but it was no use. The mastiff ran on effortlessly, until he and Pinocchio were far out of the Fisherman's reach. Then he placed Pinocchio down gently.

"How can I ever thank you?" asked Pinocchio.

"There is no need," said the mastiff, as he licked Pinocchio's face clean. "Now my own debt to you for saving my life is repaid. But if I had come a few minutes later, I'm afraid you would now be a crusty fried meal for that horrible Fisherman."

"Oh, please don't remind me!" gasped Pinocchio.

The mastiff laughed and then stretched out his paw and shook Pinocchio's hand.

"Good-bye, my friend. Now that you are safe I must go."

They said good-bye, promising each other lasting friendship.

All alone, Pinocchio walked on toward home. He soon passed a small beach cottage. An old man sat beside the doorway sunning himself.

"Pardon me, sir, can you tell me if there is any news of the boy who was recently hurt on the beach?" asked Pinocchio.

"Why, yes, you needn't worry about him. He is fine and has gone home," replied the old man.

"Oh, what wonderful news!" the puppet cried happily. Then he thought to himself, "And I can also go home!"

"Yes, but it might have been more serious," the old man continued. "A heavy book had been thrown at him."

"And who threw it?" Pinocchio asked cautiously.

"One of the boy's schoolmates, a certain Pinocchio. They say he is terrible."

"Lies, lies! This is not so at all."

"So then you know him?" the old man inquired.

"Oh, only by sight, of course. I do not know him well."

"What do you think of him?"

"Why, he is a very fine fellow indeed and quite handsome besides. His father never ceases to be proud of him. He is obedient and never lazy. . . ."

As the puppet said these words, his nose began to grow.

When he touched it, he found it had grown to more than twice its normal size, while the old man looked on with surprise.

Frightened, Pinocchio cried, "Wait! I am mistaken. All the good things I have said of this miserable puppet Pinocchio are untrue. I know only too well that he is a terrible scoundrel. A disgrace to his father, lazy and dishonest, I assure you." After this speech, his nose began to return to its normal size.

"Why are you so chalky white?" asked the old man.

Pinocchio suddenly realized how very foolish he must look still caked with flour and without his paper clothes which he had lost while swimming.

"Oh, I have fallen on hard times. It is too long a story to tell you. But if you would be kind enough to give me some clothes, I would be forever grateful."

"I'm afraid the only thing I have that is not in use at the moment is an old discarded potato sack. If it will help you, you are welcome to it."

Pinocchio gladly took the bag. After ripping a hole at the top for his head and two holes for his arms, he slipped into it. Dressed in this way, he thanked the old man and hurried on.

All the way home Pinocchio struggled with what he would tell the Blue Fairy. By the time he arrived at her cottage it was dark. He hesitated at the door, too ashamed to knock. At last he found the courage and tapped softly. Some time passed, and finally a window opened on the top floor. A large Snail wearing a miner's hat with a light on top stuck her head out.

"Who is disturbing our sleep at this late hour?"

"Tell me, Snail, is the Fairy at home?"

"The Blue Fairy is sleeping and does not wish to be disturbed. Who are you?"

"It's only me."

"Who is *me?*"

"Pinocchio."

"*Pinocchio* who?"

"Snail, it is me, Pinocchio, the puppet who lives in this house with the Fairy."

"Oh yes, now I remember. Wait a bit and I will come down."

"Please hurry. It's begun to rain and I am freezing."

"Pinocchio, you know I am a snail and snails cannot hurry. Be patient and I will come."

With that the Snail closed the window and disappeared from view. Time dragged on; at least an hour passed and the door did not open. Pinocchio knocked again. A window soon opened on the second floor and the Snail looked out.

"Who is it?"

"Dear, good Snail, it is I, Pinocchio. I am waiting here, cold and wet. What is keeping you?"

"Pinocchio, I'm a snail and snails cannot hurry." And she shut the window again.

The clock tower struck midnight, then one o'clock, then two, and still the Snail did not appear. Frustrated beyond patience, Pinocchio took hold of the knocker and began banging at the door. But as he did so the knocker turned into a slippery live Eel that wriggled out of his hand and jumped into a pool of rainwater in the street. Then Pinocchio began to kick the door with his foot. He kicked so hard his foot split the door and was wedged in the crack like a nail that has been hammered down. He was left with one foot on the ground and the other fastened securely high up in the door. He struggled to free himself, but instead he lost his balance and fell flat on his back in the muddy street, with the one foot still stuck in the door.

At long last the door opened. Nine hours had passed, and now it was a bright sunny morning.

"Pinocchio, what are you doing with your foot stuck in the door?" asked the Snail, laughing.

"I'm caught. Beautiful Snail, now that you are finally here, please get me free."

"I'm afraid we'll have to wait for the Carpenter to come get you out."

"Then please, at least bring me something to eat while I wait," begged Pinocchio.

"Very well, and in the meantime you can amuse yourself by counting the ants that pass down the street," the Snail replied cheerfully.

After three and a half hours, the Snail returned carrying a silver tray on her head. The tray contained a loaf of bread, a roast chicken, and four ripe apricots.

"Here is the breakfast that the Fairy has sent you."

Pinocchio felt comforted at the sight, but he discovered to his horror that the bread was made of plaster, the chicken, cardboard, and the four apricots, painted alabaster.

"Oh, no!" cried Pinocchio. With that he fainted.

When he awoke, he was back in his own bed with the Fairy sitting at his side.

"Fairy, will you ever forgive me for being such a fool?"

"Yes, I forgive you, Pinocchio, but I may not the next time," she said firmly.

"There will never be a next time, I promise."

Pinocchio kept to his word. He studied hard and stayed out of trouble all the rest of the year. At the end of the school term he was ready to graduate, and with honors besides. The Blue Fairy was so pleased that she decided to give him a party.

"Tomorrow your wish will finally be granted."

"What do you mean?" asked Pinocchio.

"I mean that tomorrow you will cease to be a puppet. Instead, you will finally be what you have worked so hard to be —a real boy."

CHAPTER XXIV

Pinocchio asked to tell his friends and invite them all to his party. The Fairy agreed, but she reminded him to be sure to be back home before dark. It didn't take long for Pinocchio to give the news to his friends—all except one whose name was Candlewick. Though he was lazy and mischievous, and never did a bit more work than he absolutely had to, Pinocchio liked him best among his friends. Romeo was his real name, but he preferred the nickname Candlewick because he was as short, thick, and bright as the new wick of a little night candle. Pinocchio looked everywhere for him, but no one knew where the boy was. Pinocchio went to Candlewick's house twice, but there was no sign of him. As the sun was going down Pinocchio decided to return one last time to his friend's home. There he called out the boy's name over and over again.

"Quiet. Someone will hear you," said a familiar voice.

"Is that you, Candlewick? Where are you?"

"Pinocchio, be quiet. I'm hiding under the porch. If you don't stop shouting, you will give me away for sure."

Pinocchio walked over to the porch, leaned down, and peeked in. Sure enough, there was his friend crouching down in the darkness. In a whisper Pinocchio continued, "What are you hiding from?"

"I am here waiting for nightfall. If I come out before then

someone might see me and keep me from my plan," his friend whispered back mysteriously.

"What plan?" Pinocchio asked, intrigued.

"I am going away tonight for good."

"But tomorrow I'm having a party because I will finally become a real boy, and I want you to come."

"I can't. You'll have to hold your party without me."

"Why can't you put off going for a day?"

"Pinocchio, I'm sorry, but I'll never get another chance like this again. It's now or not at all."

"What chance? Where are you going? I don't understand."

"Listen, tonight—very soon in fact—a carriage is coming to take me far away from this place, to a land called Cocaigne, where no one ever works, where boys are allowed to play all day and eat candy instead of vegetables. I'll never have to go to sleep on time, or go to school, or study. It's a paradise, and if you had any sense at all you'd join me."

"Hmmm. But I will be a real boy tomorrow instead of a puppet, and that is really something to look forward to."

"Oh, really? And what's so special about being a real boy anyway, I'd like to know. It's never done me any good, I'll tell you. Oh, listen, my friend, *no more work!* It's play from morning to night, don't you see? What more could anyone ask for! Isn't it what you always wanted?"

"Yes, that certainly sounds like the life I once hoped I'd have, but things are different now. I've changed. . . . But tell me again: What do you do all day if there is no work?"

"Pinocchio, you have studied too long. Don't you understand, one does nothing except play! You get up and you play all day long. When you feel like it and not when someone tells you, you go to sleep, and then you get up the next morning and start all over again. What do you say—do you want to come?"

"Me? No, I can't," Pinocchio said firmly. "I promised the Fairy I would be good, and I must keep my word. In fact, it's getting late and I should be home already. I promised to be home before dark and it's dark now. I must go, my friend. Have a good journey. I hope this land is all you wish it to be."

"Oh, you are such a baby. What if you're home late? What will your Fairy do? Scold you? I say let her scold. When she gets tired she'll quiet down. Stay with me a little longer and see me off. What's the harm in that? After all, we may never see each other again. Stay."

"All right," he said, "for a few minutes. When will the carriage arrive and who else is going?"

"It will come right here as soon as it's dark. There will be a hundred boys leaving tonight, I hear."

"I'd like to see that," Pinocchio said pensively.

"Well then, wait with me."

"No, the Fairy will worry."

"Poor Fairy. Ha, what does she think, that wolves will eat her precious wooden Pinocchio?"

"Stop your teasing. Tell me something: Is there no work *at all* in this land?"

"None."

"And no teachers?"

"None at all."

"And no books?"

"Pinocchio, I'm telling you, there is nothing but *fun!*"

"It really sounds like a wonderful country."

"Then change your mind and come with me."

"No, I can't. . . . The Fairy . . . would. . . ."

"Yes, yes, I know. All right then. Off you go and give my regards to all the rest of the schoolboys."

"Yes, I'm off. Good-bye."

Pinocchio took a step, stopped, and then turned back to Candlewick. "Candlewick, are you certain? No work at all?"

"Oooh yes, I'm sure."

"My, my, it does sound perfect. Oh well, I'm off. Good-bye again."

But Pinocchio couldn't resist and turned back for a second time. "Will you be going very soon?"

"Right away."

"If you're sure, I'll wait with you awhile longer."

"What about your dear Fairy?"

"Oh, she'll wait for me. I'm late already. It won't make a difference now. Either way I'm in for it."

Just then, in the distance, was the soft sound of bells and tiny trumpets.

"What's that?" Pinocchio asked.

"Here they come," said Candlewick, crawling out from his hiding place under the porch.

"Who?" Pinocchio whispered excitedly.

"The carriage, of course. They're coming. It's time for me to go! Now once and for all, are you coming with me or not?"

CHAPTER XXV

The two friends watched as the carriage drew closer. It was drawn by twelve identical donkeys. On their feet, they wore leather shoes made exactly like boys' shoes. The wheels of the carriage were wrapped with cloth to muffle any sound. The wooden carriage was brightly painted red, blue, yellow, and green, and tiny silver horns and tinkling golden bells hung from every corner. The Driver sat on top of the carriage. He was a stout man, round as a big ball. He had almost too sweet a smile. His little wet red lips curled up gaily at the corners, and his voice was soft and warm and so very friendly. No child could resist his charming ways. Once children heard him speak of the land where everything was free and filled with fun, they longed for him to take them there in his beautiful carriage.

Tonight he had a carriage crowded with eager boys. They squeezed inside, some spilled out the windows laughing, others sat huddled close together on top of the roof and hung on tightly to keep their balance. No one minded the discomfort. All they could think of was that once they arrived in paradise, in just a few hours, their troubles would be over.

Finally the carriage slowed and came to a stop in front of Pinocchio and Candlewick. The Driver climbed down from his seat with great effort.

"Oh, dear me, my dears," he murmured sweetly. "I really must go on a diet. But it's so difficult, you know, when one loves candy as much as I do."

He reached into his pocket and pulled out some rich dark chocolate.

"Here, my dears, would you like some?"

He handed them both a piece of sweet, soft chocolate and popped the rest into his mouth, licking what was left on his chubby fingers with his small pink tongue.

"Hmmm, isn't that delicious? I have lots more back at home. So, tell me, are you both quite ready? We mustn't keep the other boys waiting," he said, waving a fat little arm toward the carriage.

Candlewick spoke right up. "Yes, indeed, I am, sir!"

Wasting no more time, he moved quickly to the carriage.

"Very good, but I must tell you we are very full tonight, so you will have to find room by squeezing in with the others."

Pinocchio hung back. The Driver placed his chubby fingers lightly on the puppet's shoulder.

"And what about you, my little wooden one? Are you ready for the land you've always dreamed of? Or must you stay behind alone?"

"I must stay," said Pinocchio sadly.

"Too bad," replied the Driver, not removing his hand from Pinocchio's shoulder. "And do you have such important business at home?"

"Yes, someone is waiting at home for me, right now."

Candlewick called out from inside the carriage, "Pinocchio, come with us."

Pinocchio hung his head but didn't answer.

"What will you do then?" asked the Driver.

"Oh, you know, go to school, work hard. All those things. It is expected of me."

"Yes. Such a gloomy life though, isn't it? No one seems to have any fun in the ordinary world. Work, work, work is all they think about. Except, of course, where I come from. There it is different," said the Driver with a little chuckle.

"Is it really as you say?"

"Oh, yes. And even better than anyone can describe to you. You have a good imagination; use it! It's everything you've dreamed of. Every dream that you've forgotten and replaced with ideas of hard work. Haaa, but you know best, I'm sure," said the Driver. Still he did not remove his hand from Pinocchio's shoulder. With an affectionate pat he gently led the puppet toward the carriage, saying, "Well then, good-bye."

"Wait!" said Pinocchio with a deep sigh. "If you find a seat for me, I will come, after all."

"I'm afraid all the seats are filled, my boy. But I will gladly give you my box seat and walk myself," the Driver said.

"No, I couldn't take your seat. May I ride on the back of one of the donkeys?" Pinocchio went up to one and attempted to climb on his back, but the donkey resisted. He gave Pinocchio a kick that sent the puppet to the ground. The other boys laughed, but not the Driver. Silently, he walked over to the offending donkey, took the animal's ear in his hand, and leaned down, whispering something the others couldn't hear.

Then he turned to Pinocchio and said, "Now, try again."

Pinocchio was embarrassed and angered by the boys' laughter, so he leaped up onto the donkey. Then the carriage got underway.

While they rode along, Pinocchio was certain he heard someone crying. He looked back around, but the Driver, seeming to hear nothing, hummed contentedly to himself. None of the boys appeared to notice it, either. Then Pinocchio looked down at his donkey. To his surprise he saw that the poor creature had tears in his eyes, just like an unhappy child might have.

Pinocchio called back to the Driver. "Sir, this poor beast is crying."

"Let him cry," said the Driver, not the least disturbed. "He'll be quite happy when we get home."

At daybreak, the carriage arrived at its destination. It was everything the Driver had promised. The country was filled with boys, all the very same age. There was such noise, merriment, and shouting that it was quite enough to turn any boy's head. Some were playing ball, some were riding bicycles, and others rode wooden horses. A group of boys was playing hide and seek, and a few were chasing each other. Boys dressed up in costumes were lighting matches, some were singing songs, and still others were leaping from piles of rocks. There were boys who were throwing stones, others who were walking on their hands with their feet in the air, and others dressed as generals, strutting about wearing leaf helmets commanding squadrons of cardboard soldiers. Boys were laughing, screaming, clapping their hands, whistling, or clucking like a hen who had just laid an egg. It was such bedlam, such an unrestrained uproar that it was enough to deafen a listener.

In every corner canvas theaters had been set up, which were crowded with boys from morning till night. On the walls of every building there were inscriptions written in chalk or paint: Long live playthings; We will have no more school; Down with arithmetic; and other similar fine sentiments all in bad spelling.

Pinocchio and Candlewick had barely set foot in town before they were in the thick of the commotion. In a few minutes they had made everyone's acquaintance.

There were mountains of candy, chocolates, and sweets of every kind imaginable, and cakes and cookies all freshly baked daily—a supply that never seemed to run out. The boys helped themselves to all of this, forgetting polite manners and eating with their hands, never wiping their messy mouths. Hours, days, and weeks rushed by and crowded together to make one long, endless holiday. Candlewick and Pinocchio felt they couldn't possibly be happier.

"Well, what did I tell you? Isn't this a wonderful place?" Candlewick asked proudly.

"Yes, this is wonderful. You know, Candlewick, everyone was wrong about you. They all said you were a terrible trouble-maker who would never amount to anything and that I would be the same, if I were your friend. Well, they were wrong."

"Ah! I forgive them," said Candlewick smugly. "I suppose

I gave them enough trouble, but, poor fools, I always knew better than they what was good for me! "

CHAPTER XXVI

One morning, which seemed just like any other, Pinocchio awoke to sunlight streaming into his window. He stretched, yawned, and scratched his head. Then something very out of the ordinary took place. His yawn sounded very much like the hee-haw of a donkey, and the top of his head seemed to have two furry, floppy ears. He ran to the mirror to see if this could really be true. There, to his astonishment and terror, he saw his own familiar face, but overnight he had acquired long donkey ears on either side of his head. He began to scream and pull desperately at the donkey ears, but they continued to grow. A little Mouse heard Pinocchio's screams and crawled out from a crack in the wall.

"What's all the noise about?" he asked as he rubbed his sleepy eyes.

"I'm very sick, Mouse. Here, feel my pulse. Is it weak?"

"Pinocchio, your pulse is normal enough. I know what your problem is. I've seen it often and I'm sorry to be the one to have to tell you," said the Mouse hesitantly.

"What is it? And please, please tell me how I can cure it."

"I'm afraid there is no cure, my friend. You see, you have

what all boys eventually get when they live here," said the Mouse and then he stopped. He did not wish to continue because he liked Pinocchio, who always left him a bit of food.

"Please tell me, Mouse, what this is all about."

"Well, we call it the Donkey Disease. Oh dear, don't be too upset. Look, I'll try to explain. In a few hours you will be a donkey from head to toe, just like the fellows who pulled the carriage that brought you here."

"No, no! It can't be," Pinocchio wailed.

"Come now, Pinocchio, you must have known your fun couldn't last. What else could happen to boys who do nothing all day but play and be silly? Of course they become donkeys."

"But this is so unjust. It's all Candlewick's fault. I want to go back home," insisted the puppet.

"Are you saying he forced you to come with him? Come now, Pinocchio, no one can force you to do anything. Certainly no one was able to force you to stay home and go to school."

"That's because I haven't a bit of sense. I have always been a fool. If only I had done what the Blue Fairy asked, I would be home with her now and a real boy, instead of half a puppet and half a donkey."

"Soon, my friend, you will be a full donkey. You're beginning to grow hair already."

"Wait till I get my hands on Candlewick!" Pinocchio shouted as he started out the door. Before he left, however, he turned back and took a cotton stocking cap from his closet. He pulled the cap down low on his forehead and stuffed his ears inside to hide them. Then he ran out the door muttering angrily.

He looked everywhere he thought Candlewick might be playing, but there was no sign of him. At last he went to Candlewick's house and knocked on the door.

"Who is it?" Candlewick called.

"It's me, Pinocchio. Let me in."

"I'm sick today. Come back tomorrow," Candlewick said.

"Sick! You can be no sicker than I am. Let me in at once or I'll break the door down."

"Pinocchio, stop fooling. I really am ill. Come back later."

But Pinocchio continued to bang on the door until Candlewick called out, "All right, all right. Just give me a minute."

In a few moments Candlewick opened the door. He, too, wore a cap on his head.

"Why are you wearing a hat?" Pinocchio asked.

"I have to. It's the doctor's orders because I hurt my foot. And you, why do you have one on?"

"Hmmm, for the same reason, I think."

"Oh, no. Really?"

"Yes, my poor friend, I do believe we have been striken by the same disease. From what I hear there is no cure."

Candlewick was shocked. "What do you mean? Surely I will recover."

"Listen, when I count to three we will both pull off our hats. Then we will know if we both have the same illness," suggested Pinocchio.

Candlewick agreed, and at the count of three they both removed their hats. Astonished, they stared at each other's enormous ears. But instead of crying, they began to laugh till their sides ached, and until they heard that same curious hee-haw. At that sound they both turned deathly pale.

"Did you hear that?"

"I thought you did it."

Suddenly they fell to the floor on all fours and began to run around the room just like donkeys.

"I can't stand up!"

"Neither can I!"

Then their faces began to change and grow long. Their legs turned furry and their bodies were covered with stiff coarse hair. They tried to cry, but instead they began to bray: "Hee-haw! Hee-haw!"

Just then there was a loud knock at the door. The Driver walked into the room holding a whip.

"Well, you bray like perfect donkeys. I heard you and I've come to take care of you."

He combed each one with a currycomb. As he did, he cooed to them softly. "There, there, my darlings, don't be afraid. Soon you will be off to the marketplace. Because you are so beautiful, you will make a handsome fortune for me."

He took two bridles and, after fastening them securely around their heads, he escorted them to the market.

Just as he had predicted, two buyers were eager to part with large sums of money in exchange for such fine animals. Candlewick's fate was left to a hard-working Farmer, who took him off to his fields to work. Pinocchio was sold to a Circus Master, who planned to train the beast to jump and dance with other trained animals.

CHAPTER XXVII

Now a donkey, Pinocchio's life was hard and weary at the circus. When he first arrived the Master took him to the barn and placed him in a box stall. The man filled the manger with coarse chopped straw and told Pinocchio to eat. Pinocchio took a bite, but then spit it out. The Master spoke harshly to him and replaced the straw with some dry, moldy hay, but Pinocchio did not eat that, either.

"So, it's not fine enough for you," growled the Master.

"Well, we'll see if I can't teach you to forget your fussy taste."
He took his whip from the shelf and gave Pinocchio some sharp
cracks across the back. Pinocchio brayed out in pain. The
Master, who could understand donkey talk, knew Pinocchio
was trying to say that the hay would give him an upset stomach.

"Do you think I can afford to give you the very best hay?
You are very much mistaken," and he whipped Pinocchio again
across the back. Frightened, Pinocchio decided it was wiser to
attempt to eat the hay. As he did, the Master stopped whipping
him and left the barn in a huff. "I suppose I'll get used to it,"
Pinocchio thought between hard swallows.

Soon the Master returned. "Don't think I brought you here
to eat and drink your fill," he said gruffly. "Come along. It is
time for your training to begin."

Pinocchio was led to the circus tent and placed in a ring.
Day after day he was trained to jump through hoops, dance on
his hind legs, and make low bows. When he faltered or didn't
understand, the Master whipped him. At last the day arrived
when the Master felt he could teach Pinocchio nothing more.
A new star would be announced at the next circus show.

 PINOCCHIO THE DANCING DONKEY
Will Make His Debut Performance Tonight!

The little circus was packed with crowds of people eager to see the new performer. The Master was dressed in high, shiny black boots, tight beige riding breeches, and a bright-red jacket. He wore a satin top hat and held a whip in his hand. As he walked into the ring the audience clapped with approval.

"Tonight, my friends, you have the honor of marveling at the most unusual and talented donkey of all time." Then he paused for dramatic effect as the circus crew led Pinocchio out toward the ring. "And here he is, Pinocchio the Dancing Donkey!" Carried away by the grand occasion, the Circus Master could not resist exaggerating a bit. "Pinocchio the extraordinary, who has danced before kings and queens, will now dance for your enjoyment!" Of course, this wasn't the least bit true, but some theatrical people feel it is always necessary to dramatize a point.

The band started to play and the crowd cheered when they saw Pinocchio. All eyes were on him as he trotted out to the middle of the ring. He wore a brand-new shiny leather bridle with buckles of gleaming brass. His mane was braided with satin ribbons of all different colors. His tail was adorned with a red silk bow, and around his waist he had a girth banded with silver and gold. The crowd was so impressed they continued to cheer and applaud till the Master silenced them by raising his hands high over his head. Then he cracked his whip and shouted:

"Begin!"

Immediately Pinocchio began dancing around the ring, careful not to miss a step. The audience sat hushed by the amazing spectacle. While Pinocchio danced, the Master raised his arm and fired a pistol. The entire crowd jumped with surprise and the donkey fell down, pretending to be wounded. He rolled and lay stiff, as if dead. Then, at a signal from his Master, he rose up in one leap and began to dance again to the delighted applause of the crowd. Pinocchio looked at the many faces in the crowd as he pranced. A woman was seated in the front row. She wore a blue dress and around her neck there was a gold chain which held a locket containing the picture of a puppet.

"That is my picture! She is the Blue Fairy!" Pinocchio thought.

Overwhelmed with joy, he shouted, "Blue Fairy!"

But what was heard was only a bray. Desperately, over and over, he tried to say the words for her to understand. The audience began to laugh at him and move restlessly in their seats; now the donkey was no longer entertaining. The Master cracked his whip, cutting across the donkey's back. Pinocchio obediently tried to dance again, but when he turned to look for the Blue Fairy, she had gone. This was too much for the poor donkey. He began to weep bitterly and the Master could no longer control him, no matter how much he used his whip. The crowd started to jeer at the cruel Master and as Pinocchio was rushed away he stumbled, twisting his hind leg badly. His leg became lame and he was in such pain that the circus crew could hardly manage to lead him to his stall.

Finally, late that evening the veterinarian was called. He told the disgusted Circus Master that this poor donkey would never be able to dance again.

"Then there is no use keeping a lame donkey. Take him away and sell him for whatever you can get," the Master told one of the stable boys.

The next morning the boy led the limping donkey to the marketplace. He was sold quickly for a fraction of the price the Circus Master had originally paid.

"At least I will be able to use the skin of this wretched donkey," thought the buyer. "If it's tough enough, it might be good for a drum."

The man wasted no time. Leading the donkey, he set out immediately for a cliff that overlooked the sea. When they arrived he tied a heavy stone around the donkey's neck and attached a long rope to the stone. Then he pushed the poor donkey over the edge of the cliff into the deep water. Pinocchio sank to the bottom, and the man, still holding the other end of the rope, sat down on a rock to wait patiently for the donkey to drown.

CHAPTER XXVIII

Pinocchio, gasping for air at the bottom of the sea, struggled frantically to get free of the stone. In the distance he saw a school of fish coming his way. With each blink of his eyes they came closer, until at last they surrounded him. Those hungry fish tore at his flesh with their sharp teeth. Weighted down by the stone, Pinocchio was helpless to defend himself. Finally, when they got down to his bones they stopped and swam away. One bite of the bones, as hard as wood, had assured them there was nothing more worth eating. What actually was left was the wooden puppet body of Pinocchio. When he recovered from the shock of still being alive and back to his original self, he quickly unfastened himself from the rope and left it tied to the stone. Then he swam off.

"I know this was the work of my Blue Fairy. She sent that school of hungry fish to free me from my donkey form when she knew I was in danger of drowning," he told himself.

When he came to the surface he was too far off to be noticed by the man who had bought the donkey. But he could see the man struggling to pull up the stone. "Won't he be disappointed when he finds what's at the other end of that rope," the puppet said, laughing.

Then Pinocchio swam on in the opposite direction. Up ahead on a rock he saw a lovely little Goat, bleating. It seemed

to be beckoning him to come nearer. As Pinocchio got closer he could see that the pretty little Goat's fur was not white but a beautiful pale blue. At once he realized it was his Blue Fairy. Pinocchio was filled with joy, and he began to swim as fast as he could toward her. At that moment the little Goat screamed out a warning. When Pinocchio looked behind him he saw the terrible teeth of the giant sea monster, the Dogfish, coming straight for him. He had no time to think, but continued to swim as fast as he could in the little Goat's direction. She came to the water's edge and stretched out her leg to hoist him up as soon as he approached, all the while crying out to him to hurry.  The puppet tried to pick up speed, knowing that if he failed, in minutes the Dogfish would gain on him. Just as he began to near the little Goat he felt himself being drawn backward with tremendous force. The sea monster had opened his gigantic mouth, filled with hundreds of yellow razor-sharp teeth, and had begun sucking in gallons of water. Everything was being drawn in, including Pinocchio, and he was helpless to fight against the pull. Suddenly he was in darkness as black as ink. Now and then a gust of wind blew him backward, and the hollow sound of the echoing wind was all that seemed to surround him. Slowly he began to realize he was a prisoner inside the stomach of the dreadful giant Dogfish and that the wind was the monster's breath.

Again he had lost his chance to be with the Blue Fairy.

This time he was certain he had no hope of ever seeing her again. He began to cry and call out in the darkness.

"Who's there?" answered a tiny hoarse voice.

There in the darkness Pinocchio could just make out a Tunny that also had been pulled in at the same time.

"My name is Pinocchio."

"What sort of fish is that?" asked the Tunny.

"I'm not a fish, I'm a puppet. Can you tell me how to get out of here?"

"There isn't any way at all. We will just have to wait here to be digested," said the Tunny with a sigh of resignation.

"Digested! I don't want to be digested."

"Well, it can't be as bad as being caught by a fisherman and packed in a can with oil," the Tunny reasoned philosophically.

"Don't be ridiculous. Of course it's as bad!"

"That's my opinion and I'll thank you to respect it, even if you don't agree," said the Tunny indignantly.

"All right, all right. But I want to get out of here. Is this Dogfish very big?"

"*Big*? He's as big as two miles, if I were to venture a guess, and I'm not even counting his tail."

While they talked Pinocchio thought he saw a flickering light in the distance.

"Do you see that light out there?"

"It's probably someone who is also waiting to be digested, nothing more."

"Well, I think I'll go have a look, all the same," said Pinocchio. "Do you want to come along?"

"No, thank you, I'd just as soon stay behind. Good-bye then and good luck."

"Good-bye. But will I see you again?"

"Who can say? It's best not to think about that."

CHAPTER XXIX

Pinocchio stumbled through the darkness toward the flickering light. As he did his feet sloshed through oily water that reeked of decaying fish. When he arrived at the source of the light, he blinked in disbelief. A candle was stuck in the neck of an old bottle at the center of a small table. An old man with a flowing white beard and long gray hair sat on a chair at one end eating a meager meal. Pinocchio was overwhelmed to realize the old man was his father, Geppetto. He tried to say something, but he could only choke back a sob of joy. He rushed to Geppetto, who recognized him immediately, and the two embraced.

"Pinocchio!" Geppetto cried through tears of joy. "Am I dreaming! Are you really here?"

"It is I, Father!"

Between tearful hugs and kisses, Geppetto told Pinocchio how he had been captured by the monster fish and had been imprisoned for two long years. He had hidden in a far corner of the huge monster. There he found a wrecked ship that the creature had swallowed, containing food and provisions that had lasted him all this time. However, his food had just about run out. He was resigned that this day was to be his last.

Pinocchio told Geppetto everything that had happened to him during his long journey, finally ending with how he had lost his chance to become a real boy.

"The Blue Fairy has been the one who really believed in me."

"The Blue Fairy?" Geppetto questioned. "Who is she?"

"She has tried to look after me and has been like a mother to me, even though I haven't deserved the love she's given me. Just when I might have become a real boy, I ran away to a land that promised nothing but fun and no work. She would never have approved, but I thought I knew better than she. Well, I was wrong. For my stupidity, I was turned into a donkey and used by a cruel master, till I became lame. Then I was sold to a man who wanted my donkey skin for a drum. When he tried to drown me, I thought I was finished for sure, but the Blue Fairy took pity on me again. She sent a school of hungry fish to eat my donkey flesh. When they got down to bone they discovered my very hard wood instead—wood that you, Father, were good enough to make me out of! They didn't like that at all. So they swam away without so much as a thank you. I could be with her now because when I swam to the surface of the water, once the fish had done with me, I saw her. I believe she had taken on the guise of a lovely blue Goat, and she called to me to come to her. It was then that I finally realized that she's always been there in different ways to guide me. Just as I was about to reach her, however, the horrible Dogfish attacked. I tried to escape, but he caught me. But if I had known that I would have to be swallowed by this monster to finally find you, Father, I would gladly have let him take me."

Geppetto was amazed by Pinocchio's story.

"Well, at least now I can die happy, knowing my dream of finding you has come true."

"Die!" Pinocchio shouted. "No, I won't let you die! We will find a way out of here."

"There isn't any way, my boy," Geppetto said, shaking his head sadly. "I am without food and soon even this candle will burn away. Then we'll be left in total darkness to starve to death."

"Never! I have an idea. . . ." Pinocchio paused and thought for a moment, then he began to speak with great conviction. "With this candle we'll get out the way we came in. Through the monster's mouth! Then we'll swim to safety."

"It's no use, I can't swim. No, I'm just a weak old man. But you are brave and might be able to save yourself. Take the last of the candle and go while you can."

But Pinocchio refused. "I won't go without you! I can swim and I will carry you on my back."

"How?" asked Geppetto, surprised by his son's bravery. "I will be too heavy for you. If you try to save us both, then you too will drown."

"No, Father, you must do exactly as I tell you. I *won't* leave you." Pinocchio was so insistent that finally Geppetto agreed.

They crept forward, holding tightly to each other's hand. Pinocchio went first, using the tiny candle to light the way through the belly of the great fish. It was a long, difficult walk, but the monster was sound asleep and it seemed nothing would stir him. They tiptoed through the length of the stomach and finally arrived at the Dogfish's throat. Fortunately the monster slept with his mouth open. Pinocchio could see between the rows of sharp yellow teeth to calm water and a beautiful patch of starry moonlight.

"Now!" Pinocchio whispered. "Now's our chance. Quick!"

They climbed up through the throat and walked slowly and ever so quietly along the monster's tongue. But just then the great fish sneezed. The impact sent them hurtling back to the bottom of his stomach once again. The very worst of it was that, in their tumble, they had lost the candle.

"Now what?" Pinocchio asked himself, but he was not discouraged, not yet.

Geppetto groaned, "We are lost."

"No! Take my hand. We can't give up," Pinocchio said, determined.

They retraced their steps and, despite the darkness, Pinocchio led them back through the rows of sharp teeth. Then he gave the signal for Geppetto to jump. Together they leaped into the water. Pinocchio felt the cool water all around him with great relief, but he didn't waste a moment before swimming to his father. He helped Geppetto hold on to him while the monstrous Dogfish continued to sleep undisturbed.

CHAPTER XXX

The moonlight aided in guiding Pinocchio, while Geppetto clung onto him tightly. They swam on for miles without sighting land. To give them both courage, Pinocchio told his father he was sure land was nearby, but in fact he wasn't at all sure. It was a hard struggle to keep afloat, and he used all his

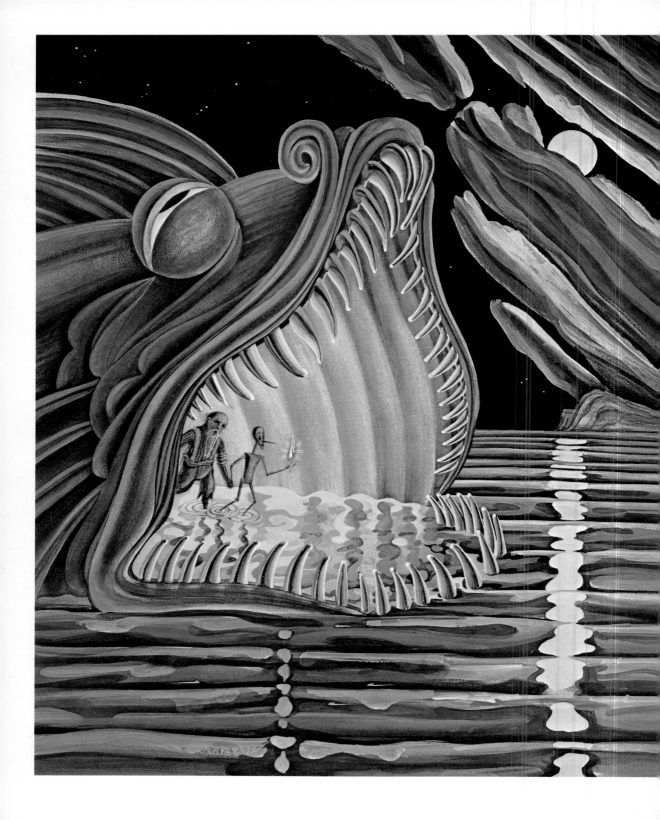

strength to do it. Soon his legs ached and he began to realize he couldn't sustain his efforts much longer. Finally, even Pinocchio began to lose hope as hours passed, and still they saw no land. Exhausted, he felt himself sinking.

"Father," he cried weakly, "I'm sorry, but I think we will drown."

"Who is going to drown?" a small, hoarse voice asked.

"My father and I," Pinocchio said desperately.

"Don't worry, Pinocchio, I'll save you," said the voice.

It was Tunny, who had been imprisoned in the stomach of the monster. He swam to their side and allowed them to grab on to his tail.

"How did you get out?" asked Pinocchio.

"I followed you both. When you jumped, so did I."

"Are we too heavy for you?" asked Pinocchio.

"Not at all. You feel as light as two tiny seashells attached to my tail. If you hold tight, I will swim you to shore."

The Tunny was a large fish with tremendous strength. He carried them effortlessly through the deep water, and in no time brought them swiftly to safety. Once in shallow water, Pinocchio and Geppetto could wade to the beach. The Tunny stuck his large head out of the water to say good-bye.

"I can never thank you enough for saving us, dear Tunny. Please let me give you a kiss."

The Tunny was embarrassed and blushed, but he was delighted to allow Pinocchio to kiss him on the head. Their eyes were filled with tears as they said good-bye, and they promised to remember each other always. Then the Tunny swam back through the deep water to his family, while Pinocchio helped his father toward the sandy beach. Geppetto was much too weak to walk on alone, so Pinocchio let his father lean on him for support.

The exhausted Geppetto asked, "Where will we go?"

"Don't worry, Father. We'll stop at the first house we see and ask for shelter."

They had not gone very far when they came upon two wretched-looking characters—none other than the villainous Fox and Cat. Pinocchio scarcely recognized them. The Cat had feigned blindness for so long that now he actually was blind. The Fox seemed truly lame, and he no longer possessed his beautiful long tail. In fact, they had fallen on such bad luck that the Fox had been forced to sell his tail to a traveling peddler, who bought it to use as a dustmop.

"Pinocchio, our dear friend," cried the Fox, "you must help your good friends. You must give us some money."

"Money for your friends," echoed the Cat.

"Don't waste your breath on me, imposters! Friends indeed," Pinocchio said indignantly, turning away. "I have no money, and even if I had you would not get me to believe your lies again." And with that Pinocchio hurried Geppetto away.

"Who were those dreadful characters, my son? They called you friend."

"Yes, Father, I once called them friends also, when I was too foolish to tell good from bad. They used my greedy dreams to fill their own pockets with gold. But those mistakes can be put behind me, so long as I remember what I have learned from them. What is important now is to get you to some shelter so you can rest."

At last Pinocchio led his father down a winding road. On either side farmland stretched for miles. Finally they came to a small stone farmhouse. Pinocchio knocked at the door.

"Who's there?" someone called from inside.

"Please help us. My father and I are two weary travelers," Pinocchio begged.

"Turn the latch and come in," replied the voice.

Pinocchio did as he was told, though when they entered they saw no one at all.

"Hello? Where are you?" Pinocchio called.

From the wall in the far corner of the room he heard a familiar voice. "Here I am." It was the Cricket.

He told them that a lovely blue Goat had given him this house just yesterday. Pinocchio asked where the Goat was.

"After she gave me the house, she went off sadly, saying that her poor Pinocchio had been swallowed by a monster fish," said the Cricket.

"Will she come back?" the puppet asked.

"No, I don't think so."

Pinocchio was heartbroken. He could only think that once again he had missed his chance to see the Blue Fairy. He wanted to go in search of her immediately, but he remembered his father and he asked if the Cricket would let them stay.

"Why should I help you? Didn't you try to kill me?"

"You're right, Cricket. I don't deserve your mercy or your hospitality. Drive me away with a mallet if it pleases you, but please help my father. He has done you no harm and is too weak to go any farther," pleaded Pinocchio.

"No, you can both stay. I'll show you kindness, but see to it you do me the courtesy of treating me respectfully in the future."

"I will, Cricket, and thank you," the grateful Pinocchio replied.

He helped his father to bed and then asked the Cricket where he might find some milk to restore Geppetto's strength.

"Down at the next farmhouse there is a Farmer who owns cows. He will give you milk."

Pinocchio did not stop to rest, but instead went off in

search of the Farmer. When he arrived the Farmer told him the milk would cost five cents.

"But I have no money," said the puppet.

"You'll have to work for it, then."

Pinocchio agreed, but asked, "What can I do?"

"Well, it just so happens that my donkey has gotten sick and is unable to work at hauling water for my vegetable garden. You could take his job," suggested the Farmer.

Pinocchio agreed and hauled a hundred pails of water for the Farmer's garden. When he had finished, late in the day, he asked if he might see the donkey. The Farmer took him to the barn, and there Pinocchio saw a frail animal stretched out on the ground, too weak even to raise his head. Pinocchio knelt down beside him. He still remembered donkey language and asked the donkey who he was. He was shocked to learn it was Candlewick, his old friend, now worn out and dying. His eyes filled with tears to think that perhaps if he had come sooner, he might have been able to help. The poor donkey shook his head and seemed to smile weakly. He knew he was beyond hope, but he was glad to see Pinocchio, who loved him, one last time. He stretched his head down on the ground; his shining eyes became dull; then he gave a little shuddering sigh of relief and was gone. Pinocchio placed his head on his friend's neck and wept.

"You certainly seem to have been very fond of that animal," the Farmer said later.

"Once we were friends, but we weren't wise enough to help each other and now it's too late," said Pinocchio as he wiped his tears with his shirt sleeves.

The Farmer gave him the milk, and they both agreed that thereafter Pinocchio would return each day and work at the well hauling water in exchange for a bottle of milk.

CHAPTER XXXI

Pinocchio continued to work for the Farmer, and in addition to drawing water from the well for the vegetable garden, the Farmer taught him to weave baskets. He learned quickly and, between the two jobs, he managed to support Geppetto and himself. In the evenings he studied from a secondhand school book he had bought. He taught himself to write, using ink he made from the juice of blackberries and a pen he made from a discarded piece of scrap metal. When he wasn't working or studying, he took Geppetto out in a wagon for sun and fresh air. Soon his father began to recover. The milk and rest helped him tremendously. Once Pinocchio learned to read, he was eager to read to his father at night. When he had earned enough money for everything they needed, Pinocchio decided to buy himself some new clothes. The next day he took his savings and went to the market. There he heard a familiar voice calling, and a large Snail came up to him.

"Pinocchio, do you remember me? I tended the door for the Blue Fairy. Remember? I was slow in coming and you rammed your foot in the panel of the door. What a time we had getting you free," the Snail said, laughing.

"Oh, I *do* remember. Tell me, how is the Blue Fairy?"

The Snail shook her head sadly. "I'm sorry to have to tell you that she is very sick. She never sees anyone and now we scarcely have money for food."

"Oh, my poor Fairy. Here, Snail, you must take this money." Pinocchio gave the Snail all his savings. "This is all I have right now, but if you meet me here in a few days, I will have more for you," he promised.

"Don't you need it yourself?" the Snail asked hesitantly.

"No, my father is provided for and I can make more money. This was only for some new clothes, but they aren't important."

The Snail thanked Pinocchio and rushed off. Pinocchio couldn't believe that she was capable of such speed.

When Pinocchio arrived home, Geppetto asked him where his new clothes were. Not willing to boast about his generosity to the Fairy, the puppet merely said that he had

changed his mind and that his own worn clothes could certainly last him awhile longer.

That night Pinocchio worked very hard, weaving twice as many baskets as usual. As he worked, his mind was filled with thoughts of the Blue Fairy. Now that she needed his help, he was determined to do all he could. He didn't go to bed at all, but instead, worked throughout the night. When he finally stopped it was nearly dawn, and he was too tired to even get up from his chair. He shut his eyes and tried to recall the Fairy's lovely face. Suddenly he imagined her hand on his shoulder. Then he thought he heard her speak gently to him. "Pinocchio, I am very proud of you. You have learned well. You are good to your father and have developed a kind and generous heart. For these reasons your greatest wish will be granted you."

Pinocchio felt her kiss him on the forehead. When he opened his eyes he was alone, but he wasn't quite sure if he had dreamed it or if it had actually happened.

He got up and went to his room, and there on his bed he found a new suit of clothes and a small ivory purse. In the purse he found forty gold coins and a note. It read:

Dear Pinocchio,

We will meet again soon. In the meantime, please allow me to reward your generosity and accept these gifts I have left you.

Love,
The Blue Fairy

Pinocchio had given forty copper pennies to the Snail, but the Blue Fairy had returned the money in gold! He put the new clothes on and then went to the mirror to see how he looked. To his surprise he saw not a puppet at all, but a handsome boy with bright, happy eyes and dark, wavy hair. He thought, "I'm handsome!"

Pinocchio ran to find Geppetto, who this morning was up and out of bed. He felt so well, in fact, that he had begun to work at his woodcarving again.

"Father! Look! Look how I've changed!"

Geppetto hugged Pinocchio. "This is a miracle," he exclaimed. "Because you have brought so much happiness and good to those you love, you have been greatly rewarded," Geppetto said wisely.

"But where is my old puppet body?"

"There he is," said Geppetto, pointing to the chair where Pinocchio had worked the night before.

There sat the wooden puppet. Its head had fallen to one side and its arms and legs hung lifeless, with its feet pointed off in two different directions. Pinocchio looked at the puppet for a few moments and then said, "How foolish I have been. There can be nothing better than how I feel today since now at last I am a real boy."